"I Don't Need A Keeper!" Ginger Exclaimed.

"But maybe *I* need to care for someone." Michael surprised himself with his words. "It's kind of nice to be needed occasionally for something besides writing checks."

"Is that what your life is like?" She stared into his eyes, seeing the yearning reflected there.

"More often than not. I built it that way. Now I'm not sure I haven't made a mistake."

Ginger shouldn't have wanted to understand him. She should have been beating a hasty retreat. But she continued. "Why would you do that to yourself?"

"Probing for the dark secrets of my past?" he asked, striving for a lighter tone.

"Maybe I'd like to know the man who kisses me as though he means it."

"Oh, I most definitely mean it." Michael reached across the table to take her hand in his....

Dear Reader:

It's October and there's no stopping our men! October's *Man of the Month* comes from the pen of Leslie Davis Guccione, whose books about the Branigan brothers have pleased countless readers. Mr. October is Jody Branigan, and you can read all about him in *Branigan's Touch*.

Coming in November is *Shiloh's Promise* by BJ James. You might remember Shiloh from his appearance in *Twice in a Lifetime*. We received so much positive feedback about this mesmerizing man that we knew he had to have his very own story—and that he'd make a perfect *Man of the Month*!

Needless to say, I think each and every Silhouette Desire is wonderful. October and November's books are guaranteed to give you hours of reading pleasure.

Enjoy!

Lucia Macro
Senior Editor

SARA CHANCE

WITH A LITTLE SPICE

SILHOUETTE *Desire*

Published by Silhouette Books New York

America's Publisher of Contemporary Romance

SILHOUETTE BOOKS
300 East 42nd St., New York, N.Y. 10017

ISBN: 0-373-05524-2

First Silhouette Books printing October 1989

Printed in the U.S.A.

Books by Sara Chance

Silhouette Desire

Her Golden Eyes #46
Home at Last #83
This Wildfire Magic #107
A Touch of Passion #183
Look Beyond Tomorrow #244
Where the Wandering Ends #357
Double Solitaire #388
Shadow Watch #406
To Tame the Wind #430
Southern Comfort #467
Woman in the Shadows #485
Eye of the Storm #500
With a Little Spice #524

Silhouette Intimate Moments

Fire in the Night #299

SARA CHANCE

lives on Florida's Gold Coast. With the ocean two minutes from home, a boat in the water behind the house and an indoor swimming pool three feet from her word processor, is it any wonder she loves swimming, fishing and boating? Asked why she writes romance, she replies, "I live it and believe in it. After all, I met and married my husband, David, in less than six weeks." That was two teenage daughters and twenty years ago. Two of Sara's Desires, *Her Golden Eyes* and *A Touch of Passion*, were nominated by Romantic Times in the Best Desires category for their publishing years. And *Double Solitaire* was a Romance Writers of America Golden Medallion nominee.

One

———

Ginger Bellwood paused at the top of the stairway, knowing that there was no chance she would be able to leave the house in a pair of cream slacks and a pale green cotton shirt without Tilly seeing her. Tilly would no doubt remind her that the casual outfit was not the sort of thing a Bellwood-Lynch wore to a business meeting, even if it was with one's own godfather. At twenty-nine, Ginger was too old to be scolded, but that wouldn't save her. Although Tilly was officially the housekeeper of Bellwood Ridge, the older woman was the closest thing to a mother that Ginger had ever known. Ginger hated disturbing her peace, but today she felt like ignoring the usual traces of her existence. For six months, she had been the model of the sole surviving heir to the Bellwood-Lynch fortune. But this morning, with one of her dreams about to be realized, she was in the mood to celebrate, to momentarily pretend that she was an ordinary woman, without the responsibilities that sometimes seemed so oppressive.

Ginger looked at the gleaming banister on which her hand rested, suddenly remembering a child who had wished with all her heart to slide down the long curve without worrying that her cold-natured father would discover her enjoying herself. The temptation was too much to resist, and the need to rebel was stronger than all the lectures on deportment that had been drummed into her head. Hitching up one hip, she rested it and most of her weight on the smooth railing. She smiled at the once familiar rush of anticipation. Her balance set, she pushed off, flying down the long curve with the grace of a dancer and the pure joy of a child. Tilly entered the hall from the dining room, saw Ginger and stopped, a grin tugging at her lips. Planting her hands on her hips, the housekeeper tried for a stern expression. The twinkle in her eyes made the effort almost useless.

Ginger slid to a stop, years of secret practice making the move beautifully graceful. "Since the town came through with the money for the building fund, godfather is going to let me have the land. He just called. He has the contract for purchase ready for me to sign," she announced enthusiastically.

"I knew there had to be a reason for this little performance. It's been too long since you gave into one of your impulses." Tilly's expression turned serious as she laid a hand on Ginger's arm. "You've worked so hard these last few months, talking the town council into starting the building fund for the recreation center and then tackling the Judge about that land of his. Half the people didn't even believe they could pull off this project and the other half were waiting for you to fail or to step in and buy them the recreation center outright."

"I know," Ginger returned with a sigh. Her mood dimmed with the memory of how hard it had been to show the rural, farm-oriented town her family had founded, that it was time to plan for the progress and the population growth that was being felt all over Georgia. Brunswick was crowding Lynch Creek from the south and Macon and Atlanta were just a few hours up the road.

"You did a great job," Tilly murmured.

"Sometimes I wonder if I shouldn't have funded the whole center."

Tilly shook her head. "You know the pride of the people around here. We handle our own problems without handouts. Besides there has been, and still is, quite a bit of hard feelings with some of the older members of the town for the way your father behaved. As much as they respect and like you and your godfather, the Judge, they can't forget Lyle."

Ginger's face assumed a bitter expression that no one but Tilly was ever allowed to see. "I know. Lyle didn't know the meaning of humanity. When I was little, I often wondered if he bled green blood."

Tilly squeezed her arm, then stepped away. "I never could hold with the way he treated you. Ignoring you would have been a kindness."

Ginger laughed without humor. "We both know he didn't do that. I was the showpiece. The little princess being groomed for the next prince to take over the kingdom. I often wonder why he ever let me go to college and take that degree in business."

"Honey, you didn't see your face the day you found out about that boy he brought here for you to marry when you turned eighteen. If Lyle hadn't let you have your way, you would have shaken the dust of Bellwood Ridge off your shoes and walked out forever. You've got his strength and your mother's compassion. For all his faults, your father was no fool."

"No. He was smart, all right. He just sat back and let me think I had escaped his plans, while all the time he was weaving a new plot."

"You beat him that time, too, and all the schemes after that."

"I hated realizing I was nothing more than a commodity to be sold on the merger market."

"Well, it's over now. The Ridge belongs to you. You've come into your own in the last three years and I'm proud of you," Tilly murmured consolingly.

Ginger smiled slightly as she slipped an arm around Tilly's waist and hugged her. "And you've been my greatest ally. I don't know what I would have become if you and the Judge hadn't been around to show me that there were people in the world I could trust to care enough about me without trying to manipulate me into doing something or wanting something from me just because I was a daughter of the Bellwood-Lynch dynasty."

Tilly shifted at the accolade, a faint expression of unease crossing her face.

Ginger frowned at her obvious discomfort. "What's wrong?"

"Nothing. I just felt a little pain, that's all," Tilly hurried to explain.

Immediately concerned, Ginger tightened her hold. "Where?"

Tilly slipped from her grasp and headed for the dining room. "It's nothing more than old age. Don't worry so. You want to do something for me, go out and enjoy yourself for a change. You're leading too lonely a life shut up with those business reports and financial pages. You need a man to share this big house with."

Ginger followed Tilly, stunned at the sudden intensity in her voice. "There is something wrong. This doesn't sound like you, at all."

Tilly rounded on her. "I want you to be happy, really happy, the way I have been with my Bart."

Ginger sat down without realizing it. "I don't understand the rush. What's gotten into you?"

"I've been thinking a lot lately. I'm not getting any younger. None of us is." She uncovered a dish of bacon and eggs, before pouring Ginger a cup of coffee. "You should have someone in your life. You'll be thirty shortly. It's time for you to be thinking of starting a family."

Ginger heard her words, but she was trying to see beyond them. In all the years she had known Tilly, she had never seen her so worked up or upset. "Won't you tell me what's wrong?" she pleaded, reaching out her hand.

Tilly took it, holding on tightly. "I love you, child. I don't think I ever told you that."

Ginger felt her heart stop briefly at the solemn words. She tasted fear but held back the emotion. "You've never needed to."

Tilly saw her fear and sought to relieve it. "There is nothing wrong with me. I give you my word. But I have watched you this last year. You aren't happy, not deep down happy. You go through the motions of living, now that you've got the business firmly under control. I don't want to see you waste your life. You were made for more.''

"I don't need a man for that," she argued, trusting Tilly now to be telling her the truth about her health.

"You're wrong. The right man would be your partner. He would challenge you and hold you when you needed comfort. He would care about you and you would see that he could be trusted. The Judge, Bart and I aren't enough."

Ginger searched Tilly's faded eyes, remembering all the times the older woman's counsel had gotten her on the right track. But this time she had chosen the one thing that Ginger couldn't handle. She had been burned too often by the male of the species, the self-servers her father had dangled before her as handsome traps, and those, during her time at college, who had tried to convince her that the power and wealth her family commanded meant nothing to them.

In the end she had discovered they had all lied. Even that would not have finished her need to reach out as women had done since the beginning if she had not trusted one last time, the only time she had given completely of herself. She had been so sure she was safe in finally committing herself emotionally and physically to one man. But Jess had been a bought man, her father's last attempt to gain complete control over the Bellwood millions of which she had had half since her mother's death. She had found out the truth only weeks before the wedding. She had never forgotten the lesson of loving and betrayal.

"I can't, Tilly, even for you," she said quietly.

Tilly turned her head to stare out the window, but not before Ginger had seen the mixture of pain, determination and fear that chased across her face. For one long moment, the two women sat silently. Ginger felt something change between them. She opened her mouth to seek an explanation, but she changed her mind when Tilly rose, the expression on her face once again the same one that Ginger had lived with for so many years. Ginger watched her return to the kitchen. Hurt without knowing why, she picked at her food, waiting for Tilly to join her over coffee as she usually did. She would ask her then, she decided. But she didn't, for Tilly evaded every attempt Ginger made to return to the subject until Ginger finally gave up and left for town.

"What do you mean that you sold the land to your goddaughter? I thought we had a deal." Michael Sheridan held up a hand when the Judge would have interrupted. "My option clearly states that I have first refusal." Michael's voice grew progressively softer as his usually rigidly controlled temper rose. "You know what's at stake. You approached me about relocating here. You're the one who suggested that there was land to be had at a marketable price for all parties."

"You also seemed damn interested in investing in the group that's financing the Sheridan Electronics move and the development of this town. Now, just what's going on? You know the property options we took on parcels for expanded housing and shopping and the money we have already spent to acquire them based on the purchase of your tract of land will be lost if you back out."

"I'm aware of that. But in this case, my goddaughter's needs precede yours. I made that option in good faith, not realizing Elizabeth had put some plans into

motion for the parcel that I offered you. Because of
the wording of her inheritance, she can make null any
agreement on land inside the Bellwood holdings, as
this piece is. I hold the title, but it was a gift to me
from my cousin, Elizabeth's mother, at her death. It
once belonged to the Bellwoods and the wording of the
bequest is such that the land can't be sold outside the
family unless the family has been given first refusal.

"In my own defense, I didn't think that Elizabeth
wanted the land or would care that I sold it until she
approached me about the recreation center. I could
not break the terms of the inheritance. Her claim pre-
ceded yours. Now I'm prepared to reimburse your
money, including that of the options you have taken
out on the other parcels, as well as offering reasonable recompense, as the situation is entirely my fault.
I shall, if you wish, even help you find an alternative
site."

The Judge sat back in his chair, waiting. So much
hinged on Michael's response to his suggestion. His
plans had been carefully conceived and stealthily im-
plemented over the last year. So much was at stake.
Ginger's happiness and security meant more to him
than the risk he was running in trying to secure both.

Michael inhaled sharply at the handsome offer. His
assistant, Charles Duncan, shifted in the chair next to
his. Michael ignored Charles, to stare at the man he
had been fool enough to trust. It had been a long time
since he had been so mistaken.

The Judge faced him without flinching, easily
reading the fury held in check. "That's the best I can
do."

"You know better than I do there isn't another sec-
tion of the size I need going for sale, so don't play

games.'' Michael rose, his gray eyes glittering with anger. "I can see where a mistake could have been made, but there was no excuse for you not to let me know right away so that I could make other arrangements," he added before stalking to the door, taking great pleasure in slamming it behind him.

"Damn!" he exploded the minute he and Charles entered the elevator. "Something about this deal doesn't ring true. Find out everything you can about Elizabeth Bellwood and this recreation center and specifically when the sale went through."

"Are you thinking of buying her out?" Charles Duncan asked carefully, trying to keep pace with his employer as they exited the elevator.

"If that's what it takes to save the project. Two years have been invested in this relocation. I won't have my plans ripped up at this late stage." He swore again, his face tight with frustration. "I should have smelled a rat when he approached me last year. He asked questions about everything but my shoe size, things that had nothing whatever to do with the group we were forming or my professional life."

"You couldn't have known, then or now. The Judge has an excellent reputation. His word has always been his bond," Charles hurried to explain. "It really could have been a mistake, as he says."

"Maybe," Michael muttered, thinking hard. He had been too long in the business arena not to take the measure of every man he dealt with. Something was definitely in the wind. He just couldn't figure out what.

To anyone watching, the two men were a study in contrasts. Michael was lean, with an intensity about his expression that never varied, never allowed for

mistakes, obstacles or impossibilities. His worst crit-
ics considered him driven to scale the ladder of success; his staunchest allies found him scrupulously fair
and improbably honest in a world governed by those
who made an art of gray areas and rule-bending. His
eyes were pale gray, his hair black as the midnight.

Charles was blond with hazel eyes and a wide open
smile that invited the world to laugh with him. He had
come into the position as Michael's personal assistant
by virtue of hard work and despite his moneyed background. If Michael had all the drive, Charles had the
lion's share of the visible charm. They were friends, at
least as much as Michael permitted.

"I want that site. We *need* the land, this town needs
the jobs we can bring and our people need the subur-
ban atmosphere. Our team thoroughly researched the
best possible choice for a southern branch of Sheridan Electronics. One crazy, do-gooder spinster is not
going to throw a monkey wrench in my plans."

"Maybe we can get her to look somewhere else to
build her recreation center. I mean, if we explain how
vital this property is to us..." His words trailed off,
on seeing Michael was paying little attention to him.
Charles sighed as he followed Michael to the front entrance.

Michael stepped onto the street, ignoring the fur-
nace blast of summer heat that assailed him. He had
to have the Lynch Creek property. His present location in Maryland made a good corporate headquarters, but the factory facilities were no longer adequate.
Lynch Creek was within easy distance of Atlanta and
the town had few zoning requirements to discourage
builders. In short, Lynch Creek offered an ideal site

for a man looking to expand an already large business.

One woman, Elizabeth Bellwood, stood in his way. His eyes narrowed against the sun's glare, he walked down the hot sidewalk toward his car. The sudden impact of a body colliding with his drove the air from his lungs. Reflexively, he wrapped his arms around the figure draped against his chest.

"Damn." Orange curls filled his mouth at the oath. Two open-toed sandals planted themselves squarely on top of his Italian loafers. Sputtering inelegantly, to rid himself of a mouth full of hair, he glared into the most unusual eyes he'd ever seen. They were the color of jade, deep green, and so cool that the soaring temperature around him suddenly dipped to winter level. Startled by the collision, and the way those eyes made him feel summed up and dismissed, Michael was slow to untangle himself.

"Why don't you watch where you're going?" he said irritably.

Ginger swallowed hard, feeling the breath return to her body. His arms were strong, and were supporting her in a very awkward position. For an instant she had the oddest feeling that she didn't want to move. Then the drip of something cold and wet slid down the front of her blouse. She blinked, banishing the strange feelings and focusing on the practicalities of her situation. "You had better let me go," she murmured, peering down at the nonexistent space between them.

"I can't. You're standing on my foot," he returned dryly, hearing but ignoring the stifled choke of amusement from Charles.

"Oh!" Ginger eased off his shoes, her eyes trained on the front of his shirt. Maybe if she were careful most of the ice cream would remain on the cone. Her luck ran out. All three scoops were plastered across the expensive dark suit, the light blue silk tie and once white shirt. Her first ice cream in months and she had to ruin it by dumping it all over a man.

Caught by his assailant's utter stillness and fascination with his body, Michael stared down at himself. The garish, mounded splotches of pistachio green, bing cherry purple and gooey chocolate lay like combat medals on his chest. As he watched, two of the blobs surrendered to gravity, the sickly chartreuse one lodging at his belt buckle and the brown mess with the odd whitish lumps landing with a dismal plop on the tip of his right shoe.

"I'm sorry," Ginger offered automatically, studying the melting rocky road scoop perched drunkenly on his shoe. It had been so good, too. This was not turning out to be her morning. She nudged the scoop with her toe, hoping to dislodge it—a mistake, as it slipped between the shoe and Michael's ankle.

"Good God, woman!" Michael growled, goaded by the sticky feeling that was seeping through his clothes and now wrapping around his ankle. Shaking his foot, the chocolate went flying to land with a splat about three inches away from Charles. He jumped back, colliding with a parking meter.

Michael divided his irate frown between the bumbling Charles and the woman who had caused the debacle. "Of all the idiotic stunts," he snapped, focusing the full force of his temper and frustration on the elegant face that showed almost no emotion.

Suddenly he was aware of the sweat dripping between his shoulder blades and the scene being acted out on the sidewalk in full view of any passerby. The combination was the last straw. He should have known better than to expect rational, civilized behavior from these rural farmers. Normally he was not a prejudiced person, but after having endured down-the-road-a-piece directions, sales that abruptly became no-sales, and "out fishing" signs on local offices that should have been open, he was in no mood to be reasonable.

"It wasn't idiotic," Ginger replied matter-of-factly. "You barreled out of the building without looking where you were going." She drew back, glancing down at herself. "I'm in no better shape than you, if you'll notice."

Michael noticed all right—too much. The ice cream had managed to turn a perfectly ordinary blouse, admittedly a pretty green shade, into an outfit that a stripper would have been proud to claim. Very firm, deliciously full breasts with dark rose centers pouted against the transparent damp cotton. The shaft of desire knifing through him was as unexpected as it was unwelcome. Slamming the door on his overactive hormones, he dragged his eyes up to her face and off her delectable body.

"Woman, you're nuts," he muttered, yanking off his coat to drape it around her shoulders. He could handle temptation better when he wasn't staring it in the face. "I bet this town has a morality committee or something."

"I don't need this," Ginger argued, her temper making itself felt.

Michael nodded toward her front. "Believe me you do."

Ginger really looked at herself then and wished she hadn't. Her fingers tightened on the coat, drawing it closed. "I'll ruin it," she muttered, more embarrassed than she had been in a long time. Pink stained her cheeks.

"It's a sight better than getting arrested." He pulled a card from his pocket. "I'm staying at the hotel. You can drop off the jacket there when you get a chance."

Before Ginger could thank him he was striding away. She watched him go, surprised to find herself wishing he had stayed. Even angry, there had been something compelling about the man. She pulled the jacket closer around her, instantly surrounded by the male scent that clung to the fabric. She was crazy, she told herself as she tried not to appreciate the clean, spicy fragrance. All Tilly's talk had gone to her head. Her lips twisting grimly at the thought, she entered her godfather's office building. Maybe if she asked the Judge's secretary nicely, she wouldn't mind going across the street to the dress shop on the corner and getting her another top.

Ginger rode the elevator to the third floor, wondering what a man such as Michael J. Sheridan was doing in Lynch Creek. According to his business card, he was the president of Sheridan Electronics. She'd heard of the company and, now that she thought about it, the man. Her godfather had mentioned meeting him months ago at some business dinner in Atlanta. She reached her godfather's offices, shaking off her curiosity. She'd find out soon enough. Nothing went on in Lynch Creek that wasn't reported in full detail to everyone who had ears to hear.

The town was a piece of living American history, with its parking meters on the street, town meetings every Tuesday, a weekly newspaper that was primarily concerned with crops, the church social, the latest gossip, and the old-fashioned values of God, country, and man-woman relationships.

Lynch Creek had heard of the ERA and women's lib, but not one of the females, young or old, thought either philosophy worth the powder it would take to blow it to Hades. This was a farming community. Every person had an important role in the scheme of things. A man couldn't take care of his fields and help with the housework, raising the children or making a home. A woman might know how to run the tractors or weed, but she was too busy with her own work to become involved.

Ginger had thought, at one time, that such archaic attitudes should be updated. She had even tried and failed. Lynch Creek and its people liked their way of life, nurtured it as they nurtured the crops in the rich earth. Now she tried to help the town move into the future without changing the parts that meant so much to the citizens and, more and more, to her.

"What are you frowning for on a day like today?" the Judge's secretary demanded as Ginger entered her office. Her eyes widened on getting a good look at the state of Ginger's attire. "What happened to you?"

Ginger shrugged lightly. "A little accident with an ice cream cone." Leaving out her unusual reaction to the encounter, Ginger related the collision and her request for a replacement blouse charged to her account at the store.

"Of course, I don't mind. I won't be two shakes. You go on in to the Judge. He's expecting you," the secretary directed, collecting her handbag.

Ginger turned to the partially open door leading to the Judge's inner office. She knocked once, then waited for his command to enter. The room was furnished in antiques, not because of their value or beauty but because they had been in the same place since the Judge had opened his law firm some fifty years before. The only things that had changed were the color of the walls, the carpet and the addition of an air conditioner in one of the small windows facing the street.

"What happened to you?" the Judge demanded on seeing her.

Ginger sighed, before sinking into a chair and beginning her tale all over again. She had expected the Judge to see the humor of the situation as he usually would have. His frown was a surprise. "What's wrong? You look upset."

"I wish you hadn't bumped into him that way," he murmured finally, not answering her question.

Recognizing the evasion, Ginger's gaze sharpened. "Why?"

The Judge exhaled heavily and leaned back in his seat to study his goddaughter. "I have a bit of a confession to make about the land I'm selling you."

"What kind of confession?" Was everyone that she was close to going through some sort of odd phase? First Tilly, and now the Judge was acting out of character.

"I had another buyer for the property. However, under the terms of your mother's bequest of the land to me, you know that your claim takes precedence."

"But you've known for a while what I planned."

The Judge ignored the comment, intent on his own ends. Elizabeth's heart and sense of fair play, once touched, would effect the meeting that he needed. "Sheridan wants to relocate his factory in town, bring in some of his own people plus hire plenty of ours, build housing for them and a shopping mall, as well. Probably even more than that later on."

Startled at the plans, about which she had previously heard nothing, and curious as to why her godfather was telling her now, she asked, "Why didn't you say something before?"

"I knew how long you had been working on convincing the town they needed to plan for the future. This recreation center was the first step. I didn't think the citizens would raise the money for their share of the project. I was wrong. I ended up with both of you wanting the same piece of land. My mistake. Put it down to old age creeping up on me." For the first time in his life, he was bending the truth like a corkscrew. Ginger rarely failed at anything.

"No wonder the man was angry," she muttered to herself, knowing how she would have felt on having the rug yanked from her in such a way. Her holdings, by virtue of her father's determined pursuit of a great name, were varied and diverse. Many were scattered around the state. She was no stranger to expansion projects and options.

"He was that," the Judge agreed, watching her closely. "In his place I would have been furious. Seems a shame, too. The man is as honest a businessman as you could hope to find, and he did get the short end of the stick. Too bad there isn't something we can do to even the score a tad."

Ginger stared at him. "What are you getting at?"

"I don't like breaking my word."

"Get to the point, Godfather. You're planning something. I can tell."

He ignored the faint accusation to get to the second part in his campaign. His first had been getting Michael to visit Lynch Creek. "You've got that tract outside of town. You know the one that's too dry to farm without irrigation. That piece has been nothing but a headache for years."

"So?"

"It would make a perfect factory location."

"Why should I sell to him? Did he mention something about an alternative?"

"No, but I think his move would be good for all of us." The Judge rose and paced to the window, his back to her. "Sheridan has an excellent reputation. He was looking at other sites closer to Atlanta. I pulled strings to set up options on land around here. You know most of it is producing and the owners don't want to sell. Sheridan took out the options."

"Supposing I did offer him the land. We both know there would have to be a lot more done to it than the piece I bought. He may not even want it." She stood up, restless without knowing why. She turned, studying him closely. "Are you sure that's all there is to this deal? It isn't like you to make a mistake like this." She searched his face, suddenly realizing that her godfather appeared visibly older. Worried, she took a step toward him, then stopped, remembering they didn't keep secrets from each other. If there was something wrong he would have told her.

"Now, what could I be leaving out? And why? I was just thinking out loud. No harm in that is there?"

Ginger shrugged, feeling foolish for entertaining, even for a moment, any doubts. She only had two people, Tilly and the Judge, whom she could trust completely. Neither would ever use her or hurt her.

They loved her as she loved them. "No, of course not," she agreed, dropping a light kiss on his wrinkled cheek. "And, for you, I promise I'll think about what you said."

Two

Ginger started home, deep in thought. The Judge's idea had merit, but she wasn't in the habit of acting on anyone's judgment but her own especially when it concerned Bellwood land. Suddenly she stopped the car, reversed and made a turn on the narrow road leading to her drive. She wanted to see the acreage that was lying idle. Twenty minutes later she was parked on a ridge overlooking a wide field that was rarely cultivated. The soil was rich but dry. There was good water nearby but it was almost eight hundred feet down, and the parcel was all rolling hills with little in the way of trees. Irrigation made a harvest possible but not financially feasible. The land was also nearly four miles from town. She had been toying with the idea of putting in pulp trees, another of the main crops in the area. Her father hadn't considered it worth the effort.

Sighing, her eyes squinted against the sun, Ginger tried to visualize a factory rising against the horizon. It was too easy. Disturbed and not sure why, she restarted the car and headed home. If Sheridan was any kind of a businessman, he had to have had an alternative site, she rationalized. But she didn't like the idea of selling off part of her heritage.

Michael Sheridan paced the small hotel room while Charles spoke on the phone. A frown etched deep lines onto his face as he measured the space with angry steps. "Well?" he demanded the moment that Charles hung up.

"Of the two other towns we looked into, and the pieces we considered, one has been sold and the other has an option on it. Unless we are prepared to go looking for another suitable town, Lynch Creek is it."

"Damn!" The oath might have been mild, but the emotions that drove it out were not.

Charles winced. "We'll either have to buy her out, or hope the Judge comes up with an alternate site as he offered."

"I'm going out to her place. We might as well see what we're up against."

"You aren't going to wait for our people to research Elizabeth Bellwood before you tackle her?" Charles questioned, his brows raised at the deviation in normal operating procedure.

Michael grinned humorlessly. "I've done a lot of tackling blind over the years. Just because I don't have to, anymore, doesn't mean I have forgotten how."

Michael stared at the mansion in front of him. The white columns, the lush green grounds, the towering oaks and magnolias and the white-painted fences looked like something out of a movie set. At any moment he expected to see a woman in billowing crinolines, parasol in hand, emerge on the veranda on the arm of a handsome male. Nothing about Bellwood Ridge indicated that it had done anything but lay in an enchanted sleep for the last hundred years. Shaking off the fanciful image, Michael swore. He wasn't given to impulses, daydreams or unproductive thoughts. He had rearranged his hectic schedule to come down to Lynch Creek, because the expansion was more important than the hundred or so other things on his agenda. He was here now, stepping back in time, for the same reason. This Elizabeth Bellwood had all but ruined his plans. He couldn't help her antiquated home, her old-fashioned town, her probably ancient ideas but he could appeal to her business sense. Under her tutelage, the Bellwood holdings had multiplied. Her father had been good at business but she was better. Everyone had his price. He only had to find hers and he could still have his factory.

His mind settled on a course of action, Michael drove the rest of the way up the drive and parked in the shade of the oaks. Nothing stirred as he got out and mounted the four wide stairs leading to the front door. The brass door knocker was engraved. He lifted the lever and dropped it twice. He was just getting ready for a third try when the door opened and he found himself staring at a slightly built, gray-haired woman in a surprisingly chic looking dress. He hadn't expected so much fashion sense in the small town.

"May I help you?"

The voice fit the clothes. "I was looking for Miss Bellwood. I was told in town that she lived here," he murmured, reassured that his image of the canny spinster was right on target. Old instincts don't die, he assured himself, putting on his most harmless expression.

"She's not here right now and won't be back for the rest of the day. If you would care to leave your card, I'll tell her that you called."

Michael hesitated, glancing sharply at the woman he had taken for Elizabeth Bellwood.

"If you don't have a card, I'll take your name and your address," Tilly continued.

Michael reached in his pocket, while he did some rapid mental calculating. One mistake was all he was allowing himself. "When exactly will Miss Bellwood be back?" he asked as he handed her a card. If he hadn't been watching her closely, he would have missed the brief pause before answering.

"I'm not sure."

She was lying. He wondered why. Had Elizabeth Bellwood left orders for him not to be admitted? His temper slipped a notch. He was not accustomed to cooling his heels for anyone.

"Why don't I stop by about seven? Perhaps Miss Bellwood and I could speak then?"

Tilly shrugged. "I don't know what Elizabeth's schedule is. I can't guarantee she'll be here."

He caught the flicker in her eyes and tallied up another lie. "I'll take my chances," he said firmly before taking his leave.

Michael alternated between anger and a desire to show Elizabeth Bellwood just who she was dealing with. First she had taken his land, and now she was trying to play least in sight. But he was a master at the game and knew a few tricks of his own.

* * *

"You had a visitor while you were in Brunswick,"
Tilly announced.

Ginger stopped on her way upstairs. She'd had a
frustrating afternoon. First she'd had to get into the
house unseen, to change her clothes for her afternoon
appointments. Even now Michael's jacket lay in the
bottom of her closet, so that Tilly wouldn't ask questions she wasn't sure she could answer. The drive to
Brunswick had taken longer than usual because she
had been so wrapped up in her thoughts she hadn't
paid attention to her speed until a very irate driver had
made his displeasure known at her meandering progress. On top of that, the estimates for the playground equipment were higher than first quoted. Then
the architect had embellished the proposed plans for
the center so that the small building which the town
had raised the money to build resembled a miniature
football stadium. The contractor had bid on a job he
hadn't expected to get, at the same time that they had
planned to begin construction. He had gotten the job
and now the town would have to look for a new,
probably more expensive, contractor.

"Did you hear what I said?" Tilly demanded when
Ginger didn't answer.

Ginger sighed, rubbing the spot between her eyes
where a headache seemed permanently lodged. "I
heard. Who was it?"

Tilly pulled Michael Sheridan's card from her
pocket and handed it to Ginger. "He was quite insis-
tent about seeing you. Said he would be back at
seven."

Ginger stared at the card, wondering if she was fated
to start a collection of these little rectangles. She didn't

need to study the bold print to bring Michael's image to mind. She remembered his anger and wished that was all she could recall. He was taller than she, with a firmness to his body that told of a man who kept himself in shape. The feel of his arms around her was still vivid, as was the delicious scent that had clung to his jacket. She didn't want to feel her body tighten in response to the memories. Michael Sheridan was a businessman, someone who had come up from nothing through willpower, hard work and a drive to succeed. Her father and those of his kind had taught her to be very careful around such men. The Judge respected Michael, but she was wary and intended to stay that way despite the unexpected attack of feminine interest for a sexy male.

Suddenly Tilly's words penetrated her thoughts. "What do you mean, he said he would be back at seven? Don't you mean he said he'd call and see if I was free?"

Tilly shook her head. "No. He said he would be back. Quite determined about it, too."

So much of her life had been spent surrounded by materialistic people who had little regard for or understanding of others' needs or wishes. Her father would have issued just such a summons, without concerning himself with whether she was otherwise engaged. Even had he known of prior plans, he would have expected her to cancel them to await his pleasure. She'd spent years learning to stand up for herself, fighting for a place in her own home and winning, although she was not without scars. She would not be dictated to by Michael J. Sheridan.

"I think I'll be out this evening. With Caro," she added, angry enough at Michael to invent a prior commitment.

"Do you think that's a good idea? From the looks of you, you have one of your migraines coming on."

Ginger bit back a snappy comment. Tilly didn't deserve the brunt of her afternoon frustration and the pain that was steadily building behind her eyes. "I do, but seeing Michael Sheridan will be worse for my head than a casual dinner with Caro." If she hadn't been in a hurry to leave, she would have taken the time to explain about the land mix-up to Tilly. "When he gets here tell him that I had plans. If he still wants to see me, he can come by about ten tomorrow."

"All right, but I think you should stay at home. I can just tell him you aren't here and to come back tomorrow. There is no way he'll be able to find out differently."

Ginger smiled grimly. "Somehow I don't think that's true. The man doesn't strike me as the type to be put off with an excuse." Pretending not to see Tilly's frown, Ginger continued up the stairway to her room. Her head felt as if forty coal miners with sharp picks were working there. She was hot, tired and all she wanted was to lie down in the dark and wile away the afternoon. What she was going to do was call Caro and see if she was free.

An hour, a shower, a change of clothes and two aspirins later, Ginger climbed back in her car and headed toward town. Caro had been delighted at the chance to share a meal, even offering to cook as long as Ginger brought a bottle of wine. Ginger pulled to a stop in front of Caro's house, a small A-frame perched on the edge of a tree-rimmed pond. The sun was setting, casting a red-gold light over the land. Flowers bloomed in a riot of color around the veranda-style overhang.

Caro came out onto the porch as Ginger shut the car door. "That was fast," she said with a smile.

"I'm escaping." Caro was her best friend and closest confidante.

Caro took the wine Ginger handed her. "From who or what?"

"Michael J. Sheridan."

Caro's golden brows rose at the response. "That fox that is staying in our one and only motel? The one who has the most gorgeous assistant that God ever created?"

Ginger grinned. She needed Caro's irreverent comments to put things in perspective. "That's the one, all right."

Caro tossed her blond head, her eyes bright with more than good humor. "Might one ask why you are hiding from one of the sexiest males that this town has seen in five years?" She poured them each a glass of wine before settling on the opposite end of the sofa from Ginger.

"I'm afraid the man and I had a bit of run in."

"Oh, you mean the ice cream bit?" Caro laughed softly, seeing Ginger's resigned expression. "I heard about it less than an hour after the fact."

"Believe me, the last thing I would have chosen was plastering both of us with ice cream, especially in view of what the Judge told me later. You know the land my mother left to the Judge, the piece I'm donating to the town? Michael had an option on the parcel, plus a few others around here, for the relocation of his factory and some other related development. My purchase of the tract blew his plans out of the water.''

Caro frowned. ''How is it that this hasn't gotten around? You know what it's like keeping a secret in this town. And I can't see the town going for this. You know what a problem it was just getting support for the recreation center, even with you donating the land. Not only that; even those of us who are for a little judicious progress won't take kindly to a factory polluting our air. I'm surprised the Judge is involved.''

''Well, he is,'' Ginger stated flatly.

''Why do you think Sheridan wants to see you? Surely he doesn't intend trying to talk you into selling the parcel back to him.''

''I would if I were in his shoes. He's bound to have a great deal of time and money at stake. Depending on the kind of investment group he's formed, it just isn't feasible for him to be doing the whole project himself—he may have come too far to draw back.''

Caro looked worried. ''What are you going to do?''

''The first thing I'm not going to do is be dictated to. He had the nerve to come by The Ridge and leave a message that he would be back at seven to talk.''

''That was not a smart move on his part, especially with you. You'd think a man as successful as he is supposed to be would have a little more finesse.''

''You would think,'' Ginger agreed. ''Anyway, I didn't feel like waiting around for his pleasure . . .''

''So you called good ol' Caro and bummed a meal.''

Ginger laughed, relaxing a little. ''Anyway, that's enough about my problems. I'll hit on a solution eventually.''

''You usually do, although some of your ideas scare me gray-headed.''

"I'm not that bad," Ginger protested lightly, seeing something in Caro's face that spoke of loneliness. She had thought her friend happy since she had rebuilt her life around her new home and business. Ginger wanted to ask what was wrong, but controlled the urge.

"We've been friends for a long time." She stared into her glass. "I was thinking the other day that it's almost twelve years. Didn't seem that long. We're both getting older. I've been thinking about settling down."

Ginger studied Caro, taking in the naked vulnerability in her eyes, while wishing she felt well enough to give Caro her best. "But you are settled. Who was it who insisted on building her own house after moving to a one-gas-station, six-church town?"

"My mother does have a way with words, doesn't she?" Caro said with a sigh. "She really hated that I wanted to move back here after she married so well and ended up as one of the premier Atlanta hostesses." She looked at Ginger. "After that last relationship, I needed healing time and new values. I thought it would be enough, but it isn't. I'm lonely and I want someone in my life. And I want children. But now I'm afraid to reach out to find them."

Once upon a time Ginger had wanted those things, too—until she had learned the price of the dreams. Now, she held back, filling her life as best she could and closing her mind to words like "children" and "home." "So what are you going to do?"

Caro laughed, but it wasn't a happy sound. "I may have already done it. At least, sort of," she added hesitantly. "While you've been running from Michael Sheridan, I've been watching his assistant. I saw him a couple of times, when he came to town to meet with the Judge," Caro hurried to explain. "He only stayed two days then and I spent most of the time trying to convince myself I was out of my mind for being attracted to a pretty face. Too much of my life has been spent trying to live down that kind of image to appreciate finding out I was as beauty-conscious as the people I've condemned for reacting the same way.''

Knowing the problems Caro had had with her extraordinary beauty, Ginger could see the problems all too well. "You've never judged people by their looks."

"I've never felt this way before, and none of my previous experiences prepared me for a good, old-fashioned case of lust at first sight—or for being too scared of rejection to do anything about the situation.''

"You don't mean that," Ginger said finally.

"I wish I didn't."

Ginger downed the last of her wine, wishing that Caro had chosen another day for this kind of a crisis. Her head was throbbing, she had Sheridan breathing down her neck and Caro needed her. "What are you going to do? You could try getting an introduction or something."

"That's not my style. My mother has the market cornered on approaching eligible men. I don't, and I don't want to learn," she stated vehemently, then sighed with fatigue. "I'm just not aggressive. I can't make the first move." She tossed off the last swallow of her wine and got to her feet. "Maybe, since they didn't get the land they wanted, your nemesis and mine will leave town. Out of sight out of mind, I hope." She started for the door leading to the kitchen. "I'm going to get dinner on the table. Talking about this is making me depressed, and I hate being depressed."

Ginger watched her go, unable to think of a single thing to do to help. She and Caro had solved their problems together for so long that she couldn't leave the situation alone. But like Caro, she didn't see a solution.

Michael arrived at Bellwood Ridge for the second time. The Bellwood house was even more impressive at sunset than it had been in the full light of day. He wondered what the woman he had come to see would be like. Would she fit this pre-Civil War setting or be a product of a more enlightened era? Charles had done his best to come up with some answers while he had been cooling his heels waiting on Elizabeth Bellwood to return. He knew now that the person who had answered the door was the housekeeper, Tilly. Elizabeth Bellwood was twenty-nine, unmarried and apparently quite content to stay that way. He also knew that her father, with whom she had not gotten along, had been quite successful until his stroke five years before. On the man's death, Elizabeth had taken over the family's vast Bellwood-Lynch holdings and had made even more of a success of her heritage than Lyle Bellwood had done. The Bellwood-Lynch name was prominent in everything from politics to pulp mills, and Elizabeth was kin to almost everyone of any importance in the state.

Michael respected business acumen and he respected power. His frustration had driven him this afternoon, but his mind was in control now. Elizabeth Bellwood, young or old, was a worthy adversary. He mounted the stairs, determined to appeal to her on a professional level. If he couldn't convince her to resell the property to him at a profit, he was prepared to offer her a share in the investment group he headed to develop the housing for the influx of workers and the shopping mall that he had in mind in addition to the factory expansion. Pleased with the possibility of success, he knocked on the door.

"She isn't here," Tilly said before Michael had an opportunity to speak. "She's out for the evening."

His temper inched up at the news. "Did you tell her I intended to stop by?"

"I told her."

Her tone was neutral, and there was nothing in her expression to strengthen his suspicion that Elizabeth Bellwood had made the engagement on the spur of the moment.

"Is it all right if I come in and wait?" He tried for politeness, when he really wanted to demand.

"She didn't say how long she would be."

Michael sighed and raked his hand through his hair. The housekeeper wasn't going to move. And unless he wanted to antagonize both women, he would have to back off. His irritation rose, but this time he controlled it. "I know I should have called and made an appointment, but I have to return to Maryland soon and I need to speak to her about a business deal."

"Why don't you call around about ten tomorrow?"

Defeat did not sit well, but he could think of no way of getting into the house without using force. With a nod and a quiet "thank you" that almost stuck in his throat, Michael turned away. He could feel Tilly watching him as he got in his car and drove away. He stared down the dark drive leading to the road, mentally chalking up the tally of defeats Elizabeth Bellwood had meted out. He didn't like the count.

Suddenly, he stopped the car under the shadow of a large tree. Elizabeth Bellwood had to come home sometime. He would wait here. If nothing else he would get a look at the woman who was leading him around by the nose.

It was late by the time Ginger left Caro's house. Her head was hurting worse than ever. The two aspirins she had taken had long since worn off and the one glass of wine she had allowed herself had done nothing to take the edge off the pain. On top of that, she couldn't get Caro's emotional situation out of her mind. Caro always had her feet on the ground, even in her worst moments. Whatever she was feeling for this stranger was definitely not her normal mode of operation. Engrossed in her thoughts, Ginger did not see the car that waited in the shadows and then followed her down the drive. The first inkling she had that she was not alone was the sound of a male voice saying her name. She spun around, too startled to be afraid. The lights from the house illuminated Michael's face.

"What are you doing here?"

"Waiting for you," Michael tucked his hands in his pockets, his eyes on her. She was not at all what he had expected. Despite the limited light, he could see she was far more beautiful than the picture he had had in his mind. There was also something very familiar about her. Even her voice reminded him of someone, although he couldn't think who. Disturbed by the sensation, he pushed it away. He had to remember why he had spent the last three hours in the cramped quarters of a rental car doing nothing but counting stars.

"I got tired of getting the brush-off. I thought Southerners were noted for their hospitality."

The insult was the last straw in an irritating day. Ginger had learned to control her emotions almost before she had learned to walk. But sometimes control took second place to justifiable anger. ''I could repeat a few very pithy remarks about brash, pushy Yankees but I have better manners and a heck of a lot better upbringing.''

Michael stared at her, feeling the sting of her words, hearing the depth of her temper. What was it about this woman that triggered his less than adept handling of himself and the situation? He was annoyed at his own behavior. If he wasn't careful, he was going to lose whatever slim chance he had of recouping his original objective. Before he could open his mouth to voice an apology, she stalked toward the house.

''Damn!'' he swore, starting after her.

Ginger swung around as he mounted the porch. ''I did not invite you in.''

''I know.'' Michael halted abruptly as the bright light on the porch fell full on her face. ''You!'' he exclaimed without thinking. ''That was you this morning.''

Ginger sighed wearily. She was aware that she had no chance of getting rid of Michael Sheridan until he had had his way. ''I guess you better come in,'' she muttered as she unlocked the front door.

Three

Michael followed Elizabeth down the wide hall to the study at the back of the house. Two walls were lined with books. A huge fireplace took up most of the third, while the fourth was floor-to-ceiling windows opening onto the veranda. A large carved desk with an impressive computer terminal covering most of its surface sat in the middle of the room. Two dark blue velvet chairs were positioned in front of the hearth. A lamp burned softly on the desk and another in the corner near the door.

"You might as well sit down." Ginger gestured to one of the chairs as she took the other. If she hadn't been nursing the migraine, she would have turned up the lights to a less intimate level.

Michael eyed her warily. She had to be aware of his reasons for coming to see her. Her attitude indicated that a more businesslike setting should have been the

order of the day. Not this . . . he glanced around, then
back at her...this friendly atmosphere. What was the
woman up to now?

Ginger leaned her head back in the chair, trying to
clear her mind enough to think. "Please get to the
point of this visit. It's late and I'm tired," she said
without opening her eyes.

Michael wasn't sure whether her bluntness was welcome or not. "I want to make an offer on the land you
just purchased," he said absentmindedly, watching her
closely for a clue to her thoughts. A second later, his
study was for another reason entirely. Unless he was
mistaken, she didn't look at all well.

"It's not for sale."

"Even at a profit?" Her voice wasn't as strong as it
had been outside, he realized. "Are you all right?" he
demanded suddenly, concerned when he should have
been tending to business.

"I'm tired." She turned her head carefully, looking
him full in the face. Somewhere between the door and
the study he had lost some of his temper. She wondered why. "It's been a long day."

"And I'm adding to it," he said, feeling a twinge of
unaccustomed guilt. Irritated that the woman could
affect him when he should have been immune, he
stiffened.

Ginger didn't deny the obvious. "I won't sell.
You're wasting your time and mine by trying to convince me otherwise. That land is in a ideal location for
a recreation center. It's relatively flat, with a stream,
some woods and a small lake. It's very well suited to
my purpose. There are other pieces of land around
here. Choose one of them." Had he been more rea-

sonable about tracking her down, she would have considered discussing her own tract.

Her cavalier attitude reignited Michael's annoyance. It had been a long time since anyone had had the nerve to dismiss him so easily. "I don't want another piece. My company and I have spent months scouting this area for a suitable place for my expansion. If my sources are correct about your expertise, I shouldn't have to tell you there are more things involved than the simple building of another factory—things like housing the workers who will be moving into the area and the increased needs in shopping and professional services."

The words were just so much chatter in Ginger's throbbing head. "Get to the point," she muttered, devoutly wishing she was alone.

His temper inched up, his speech becoming more clipped by the second. "The point is that I head an investment group. We have options on the few pieces of property available for sale. Despite the lack of visible evidence of population, very little of the land around here is not being used either for cultivation or grazing. There simply isn't anything else of the size I need for sale, as I am sure you know. If I don't have your property, the group stands to lose the options and the money already paid. Not to mention the time. Lynch Creek is ideal for our purposes. With Jacksonville less than two hours away to the south, Atlanta three hours northwest and Savannah a couple more to the northeast, we would have the best of all possible locations by land, sea and air. And from the town's point of view, we'd be bringing in people with money to spend. The school system would improve, as well as the shopping and the services."

"And I'm the one standing in the way of all this progress," she summarized when he didn't. She lifted her fingers to her forehead, massaging the steadily building ache.

Michael frowned at the gesture, seeing the pale translucency of her skin. His worry increased, his annoyance fading. "What's wrong with you?" Without thinking he rose and went to her, going down on one knee beside her chair. "And don't tell me you're just tired, because I won't believe you." He brushed his hand lightly across her forehead, feeling for a temperature. Her wince gave him a clue. "Headache or migraine?" he asked, pitching his voice low. From the way she shunned the light he would bet it was the latter.

"Migraine," she admitted, hurting too much now to care if he knew. His hand felt cool against her skin. She leaned her head against his palm, taking comfort from the faint pressure that seemed to dull the pain a little.

"You should have told me to get lost," he said roughly, still keeping his voice down. Although he had never suffered from migraines, he'd had a few humdinger headaches in his time.

"You wouldn't have gone," she whispered, too tired to curse her own weakness in letting a stranger get so close to her.

He stared at the face lying cradled in his hand and knew that she had spoken the truth. He had come here tonight to do everything in his power to make her sell the land to him. Instead he found himself wanting to help her, rather than take advantage of her obvious weakness. He had dealt with women before, and had not come on like King Arthur's favorite knight. So what was different now, he wondered, studying her face in the muted light. She was attractive rather than beautiful, and she was nothing like the women who usually appealed to him. But more than anything else, she had something he wanted very badly—and it didn't look as though she was prepared to be reasonable.

Irritated, confused and wishing he had not decided to wait for her tonight, he started to draw back. But he couldn't take his hand away. The warmth of her flesh seemed to wrap around his hand, imprisoning him with invisible bonds. Strange. He stared at his fingers against her skin. The lines of pain about her eyes and mouth weren't so deep since he touched her. Startled, he looked closer. Her breathing was easing, as though he had given her some magical relief.

"Do you take something for this?"

"No. The pills just make me dopey, without stopping the pain."

Her voice was so faint he had to lean over her to hear it. Her scent caught him then, light, delicate, a gentle drift of flowers. He inhaled deeply, instinctively, and knew he was in big trouble. As though outside himself, he watched his free arm come around her, tucking her body against his chest. Her weary sigh went right through him. His arm tightened even as he called himself a fool for caring.

"You should be in bed."

"Too many stairs."

Brilliant, Sheridan. Now what? He couldn't leave her like this. "Is there someone I can call?"

"No." Ginger burrowed deeper into his warmth. "Gone to sleep." She was barely conscious of her answers.

Michael exhaled, and tried to tell himself that he was simply helping someone who needed him. The voice shouting liar in his mind was weaker than the one giving him reasons for lifting her into his arms and liking the way she curled against him as though she belonged.

By the time he gained the top of the stairs he decided Rhett Butler must have been a muscle man. The woman in his arms weighed practically nothing, but he was breathing deeply. Was it her fragrance that had his senses demanding more of the scent? Elizabeth was soft, sweetly curved, a warm bundle of femininity, and he was thinking of things that had nothing to do with business or the hurting woman in his arms. His libido was on full alert, and he was definitely breathing hard from something other than exercise.

"Which room is yours?" he asked huskily, blessing the few saints he knew for making her so out of it she wouldn't notice the emotion in his voice. Holding Elizabeth, much less getting involved with her, was not one of his best moves.

"The end of the hall, on the right," Ginger mumbled.

Michael made short work of the distance, barely seeing the decor of Elizabeth's bedroom. His eyes were trained on the silk-draped bed, which looked like something out of the *Arabian Nights*. He stifled a groan. That's all his fantasies needed. He laid her down on the turned-back covers, easing his arms from beneath her body. The cool air, where there had been warm flesh, created a strange sense of loss. He glanced at the open door, wishing he could leave and knowing he had to make her comfortable first, as it was clear she couldn't do it for herself. He started with the easiest part, her shoes.

Ginger turned her head against the pillow, looking for and failing to find the fleeting relief that Michael's touch had given her. When his hand slipped over her throat she moaned softly.

"I'm just going to get you out of this blouse. Lie still or you'll make your head hurt more," he commanded gruffly.

Sitting down on the edge of the mattress, he slid the buttons free. The lacy cups of her bra cradled her breasts as though waiting for his caress. He made himself look at her face, hating the feeling of desire spreading fire in his blood. He was not a youth who couldn't touch a woman without being ruled by his hormones, he reminded himself. He eased the blouse from her body, lifted her in his arms to pull it completely off. Her breasts stroked his chest through his shirt. His clenched his teeth and tried to think of the property she had all but stolen from him. The image lasted as long as it took him to slide her skirt down over silken thighs. His hands were shaking as he turned away to drape the clothes over a chair. When he turned back, he allowed himself one glance of her silk-and-lace-clad body before he pulled the sheet over her. Her eyes were closed, her breathing deepening by the moment. He wasn't sure whether she was on the edge of sleep or whether the pain had escalated to such a degree that she was just drifting.

"Elizabeth Bellwood, you have a lot to answer for. Not only have you trashed my plans for expansion, but you have turned me into a voyeur," he grumbled as he headed for the bathroom for a glass of water and hopefully a couple of aspirins. For her sake, he needed to get something down her throat. For his own, he needed to get finished and get out.

"Michael?" Ginger murmured fretfully, feeling his absence.

"I'm here, where I shouldn't be," he replied, sitting down beside her again. He lifted her in his arms, cradling her against him as he held the glass to her lips. "Take a swallow and then take these aspirins, Elizabeth."

Ginger didn't have the energy to argue. A moment later, she felt his arms loosen. "Hold me for a minute," she whispered, opening her eyes enough to see his face. "It feels better when you hold me." If she had been herself, the last thing she would have asked him or any man was to give her a shoulder to lean on.

"Elizabeth . . ."

"Ginger. Friends call me Ginger." The words were hard to get out, but she wanted to say them.

"I am not your friend." His words were harsh, even as he tucked her more closely against him. He stroked her back, giving her what comfort he could.

Her brow furrowed, reality and the pain world merging just enough for her to feel uneasy. Shifting, she tried to pull away.

"Stop that," he commanded, frustrating her attempts. "You'll only hurt yourself more."

"You shouldn't be here. I'm used to taking care of myself," she said faintly.

The wistfulness in her pain-slurred voice made him soften. He found he wanted to call her Ginger. And he didn't want her to be alone. Frowning, not understanding his reaction but unable to fight it enough to pull away, he rationalized his reaction. Putting an opponent in debt was never a bad move. So for tonight

Elizabeth would be Ginger. Tomorrow she would be Elizabeth, his worthy adversary.

"Close your eyes, Ginger. I'll stay with you until you sleep."

Her eyes opened, searching for the truth, even though the muted light increased the pain. "Promise?"

"Promise."

Whatever Michael might be or think, for the moment he was telling her the truth. The knowledge was enough to cause Ginger to relax in his arms. Sleep stole over her, taking the pain, leaving only the security of being held.

Michael watched the lines smooth out along her brow, felt her limbs go limp with relief from pain. He smoothed the bright hair over her shoulder, tracing the delicate planes of her face. He had been wrong. She was more than attractive. She was beautiful, curved but with sleek lines and gentle hollows. Her skin glowed like gold satin in the light. Her lips were an enticing shape, begging to be kissed. Had she been any other woman, he could have held her all night and counted himself lucky. But he had to go. He had promised. And his words had seemed to matter to her.

He laid her gently back among the silken covers, tucking the sheet around her body. Without thinking, he bent his head and brushed her lips. Surely one kiss wasn't too much to ask for his restraint. Her sigh was sweet on his tongue. Her scent clung to his clothes as he turned out the lights and left the room. He drove back to town and his less than comfortable bed, wondering what magic she possessed to turn him from his course for even a moment. No one had ever had that power. He was no nearer an answer when sleep finally claimed him.

Ginger came awake slowly, for a moment unable to think of how she had got to bed half undressed. Fragments of memory drifted through her mind. Michael carrying her up the stairs. His hands slipping the clothes from her, tucking her into bed. Based on what she knew of the type of businessman she believed him to be, she hadn't thought him capable of any gentleness or kindness. She had been wrong. His voice had held a myriad of emotions; anger, irritation, annoyance and desire. She frowned, recalling the feeling of wanting his hands on her body, of needing him to hold her, of asking him to stay. The pain had been bad but she'd had worse migraines and not craved someone's touch. In the past, she had always preferred silence and solitude.

The phone rang. She reached for it, while still thinking about her strange reaction to Michael. His voice in her ear was a surprise.

"How are you this morning?"

A blush spread over her body, making her glad he couldn't see her. "Better. Thanks for staying with me and seeing that I got to bed all right." She got the words out, needing to express her gratitude.

Michael chuckled at her phrasing. They still had business to discuss, but one more minute of being her friendly enemy couldn't hurt. "Our acquaintance thus far has been rather unique, Ginger."

"I'm sorry about the ice cream," she added, pleased that there didn't seem to be an immediate resumption of hostilities on the horizon.

"I survived." Michael wanted to say more, but couldn't find the words.

Ginger waited, hoping he would say something. The silence lengthened.

Michael sighed. He couldn't put it off any longer. "We still need to talk about the property. I meant what I said last night."

"And I meant what I said." Ginger really didn't want to fight with him. Her godfather's suggestion flitted through her mind. Would Michael go for it?

With her refusal, his practical side took over. "You're turning down a good deal, and an attractive profit. I'm also prepared to offer you a piece of the action with this investment group." His friendly tone firmed, practicality and purpose overcoming subtlety.

Ginger felt and heard the change, responding in kind. "The last thing I need is another business interest to keep my eye on."

He inhaled sharply at the blunt comment. "I don't need anyone to keep an eye on my company or anything else I'm involved in." Irritation laced his voice.

Ginger scowled at the snappy comeback. "I was not trying to imply that you didn't know your stuff," she responded stiffly.

"Then what did you mean?"

"I'm up to my ears in corporate shenanigans already. I have more money than I'll ever spend and not enough time left to enjoy myself as it is. I *do not* want any more business interests. However, I am prepared to offer you a deal."

Michael wasn't sure whether swearing or hanging up before he really lost his temper was in order. The woman wasn't just beautiful; she was a shark in silk.

No one ever had enough money. And while she was wealthy, she wasn't mega-wealthy. What he couldn't figure out was what game she was playing.

"What kind of a deal?" he asked warily, looking for clues.

Ignoring the less than enthusiastic tone, Ginger said, "I own a piece of property outside of town, five acres larger than the site you wanted. I might be willing to part with it."

"Where, specifically?" Michael pulled a town map closer, spreading it on the round table in front of the noisy air conditioner.

"Off Cutter's Road, about three miles southwest of the county line."

Michael found the location, compared it with the original site and the properties on which he had options. The location wasn't quite as good, but neither was it impossible. "What's the price? Assuming I like it."

"The same, sort of."

Michael sighed deeply at the cryptic response. "What's the 'sort of' mean?"

Ginger stared out the windows, wondering if the lingering traces of the migraine were responsible for her impulse. "You mentioned that you had a contractor for the factory. I don't have one for the recreation center. The man I had bid another job at the same time and before we could sign an agreement."

"You can't be suggesting that I loan you mine?" He pulled the phone from his ear, wondering if he had lost his mind. Was there anything this woman wouldn't dare? First, she dumped half an ice cream store on him, snatched his land, got him into her bedroom, and now she expected his help with the project that was ruining his plans. Only in her dreams and his worst nightmares!

"I am. In fact the more I think about it, the better I like the idea. You know in all your planning you haven't allowed for the fact that while you and your people might want Lynch Creek, Lynch Creek might not want you. Think of it as a gesture of goodwill. Every person in this town has, in some way, contributed toward making this recreation center a reality. Now you and yours are going to move in and ultimately use the facilities, as well. In fact, there is one more condition," she added, warming to her theme. "The playground equipment is going to cost more than we planned, so I think our newest citizen should contribute the excess in cash."

"You're crazy," Michael roared irately. "In the first place, I don't own the damn contractor. I have no say over what jobs he'll do. And even if I did, I wouldn't help you build on a piece of property that you stole from me. On top of that, I am not contributing anything to this pet project of yours. Why should I? Because of you, my plans are in shambles and I am sitting in this dingy little motel, miles from nowhere, while work stacks up at home. On top of that, I couldn't personally care less if you get your playground or not."

Ginger listened to the tirade without a word, waiting until he had wound down. She had made an error in judgment. She had allowed Michael's treatment of her the night before to fool her into thinking he was more than a businessman who measured everything in his life in terms of profit and loss. She should have remembered the lessons her father had taught.

"Then I guess we have nothing to discuss," she said wearily before hanging up the phone.

Michael stared at the receiver in his hand, unable to believe she had cut him off. No one, in recent years, had dared to risk offending or insulting him so blatantly. Angry, he slammed the phone in the cradle and paced the room, stopping only to snap a response to Charles's knock on the outer door.

"What's wrong? I could hear you shouting from the next room."

"I was not shouting," Michael said through gritted teeth. "That crazy woman is trying to hold us up. Do you know she has a piece of property that is bigger than the one we were trying to buy?"

Charles frowned. "How can that be? Our team was most emphatic about the land we had the options on being the only parcels for sale."

"Well, they missed this one."

"But surely that's to the good. Now we can go ahead with our plans." Charles's frown deepened, at Michael's negative gesture.

"Why not?"

"That woman wants me to give her *our contractor* for *her* recreation center *and* on top of that, she wants me to make up the difference in money for the playground equipment, as a gesture of *goodwill*. Both are conditions of the sale." He threw himself down in a chair, swearing when the thing creaked then listed to one side. He jumped to his feet before he landed on the floor.

Charles sat down on the bed, having had his own trouble with the flimsy furniture in the motel. "We could get her a contractor. And the goodwill gesture wouldn't be a bad idea. Small towns are notoriously clannish. And this is a town project. I heard, at the barbershop, that even the kindergarten kids helped raise money to do the park.''

Michael stopped his pacing to stare at Charles. ''What were you doing in the barbershop? The last I heard, you wouldn't let anyone but Emilio touch your hair.''

''I needed a trim. And I figured I'd scout out public opinion.''

''And?'' Michael prompted when he didn't elaborate.

Given Michael's mood, Charles wasn't eager to impart the local gossip. ''It isn't good. I'd say we are going to need all the help we can get if we intend to relocate here. These people like this town the way it is. They were delighted when the interstate took them off the tourist route, and they have a fairly good ratio of the younger generation staying on the family farms. There's an agricultural college close by, and a good many of the kids, girls and boys, are educated there. The rest of the young people, for the most part, commute to the larger towns in the area. Very few are moving. Unlike a lot of the farming communities around the country, this one is not dying. It is not only alive and well but it is happy with its old-fashioned image and values. They won't be thrilled about the influx of people we represent, the traffic they'll bring, the money they'll spend or the services they'll need. And, from what I could gather, they definitely won't be excited about having a factory breathing pollution into their clean air.''

''We do not pollute. Our plant has more than the environmentalists require in safeguards.''

''I know.''

Michael stopped pacing. In all their calculations, they had never seriously considered the town's reaction. "I bet we'll really make some enemies if we alienate Elizabeth Bellwood."

Charles nodded, pleased to see the storm was passing. An angry Michael was not someone a sane person messed with. "I think so. She might have the reputation of being a loner, and tough to deal with in business, but there isn't a person in this town who doesn't consider her more important than the clock in the square that predates the Civil War. Her family settled this place, and she's their leader of choice—whether she wants the honor or not. And more than that, she doesn't play Lady Bountiful to the peasants. She works as hard as the most dedicated of the citizens."

Michael shot Charles a sharp look. "That sounds remarkably like admiration."

"It is. I've seen members of my family lord it over those who have less than they. It isn't a pretty sight. Miss Bellwood, for all her peculiarities, seems to realize her position in the best possible way."

"I don't call polite blackmail a desirable quality," Michael observed. "Especially when it's aimed at me."

Charles grinned, acknowledging the rueful tone. "Think of it as character building."

"Don't push it, Charles. It's bad enough I'm going to look this alternative site over when I'd rather have had the first one. It looks as if Elizabeth Bellwood will get another visit from me whether she likes it or not."

Four

Ginger eased down the stairs, trying to ignore the feeling that she should have stayed in bed. She knew from experience that wishing wouldn't make her migraine disappear. Peace, quiet and an absence of stress were the only cures. Michael's call had effectively ruined having all three. Besides, she hated inactivity, so she intended to have breakfast, then take a quiet walk in the rose garden before retiring to the study to do nothing. The sound of the door knocker being forcefully plied reverberated in her head, bringing a groan to her lips. Hurrying to stop the noise, she opened the door. The sight of Michael on her veranda was not a welcome one.

"Go away." She started to close the door on him. His hand on the edge of the panel stopped her.

Michael clenched his jaw and tried to control his temper. "No! I want to see the property you offered me, but I'll need you to direct me."

Ginger pressed her fingers to her forehead, feeling the throbbing behind her eyes starting to increase. "I can't deal with this now."

Michael read the signs of pain, feeling again the stirring of sympathy and desire that had gotten him in trouble the night before. He tried to fight both and ended up reaching for her hand. "Stop that. I thought that thing would be gone by now. Why hasn't it?" he demanded roughly.

"Because you woke me up shouting in my ear," she muttered, trying to pull away. She didn't want to feel the warmth of his touch spreading through her. She didn't want to remember that, for a moment, she had believed in his gentleness and been proved a fool.

Michael swore, something he seemed to be doing a lot of around her. "You should be in bed." He moved closer, sliding his free arm around her waist. He ignored her stiffening as her scent swirled about him, reminding him of how good she had felt in his arms.

"I hate being cooped up." She pushed at his chest with her free hand, not liking the determined look in his eyes. Her efforts were useless as he simply crowded nearer, shifting her weight.

He lifted her, smiling a little at the scowl on her face. "You don't need to direct me. I know where your bedroom is," he murmured, needing to tease her to distract himself from the soft curves pressed against him. As the night before, desire burned with unexpected strength.

"I am not going to bed," she stated, annoyed that her body was betraying her with its weakness. "I need to eat."

"All right. Which way?" He stared into her eyes, for an instant losing his train of thought over the emotions swirling in the jade depths. He could see she was caught in the same trap as he, and that she was just as confused and irritated. The knowledge brought a surprising feeling of relief. He wondered why as he shook his head slightly and tried to remember what stood between them.

Ginger read his needs as clearly as she felt her own. It was strange to look into Michael's eyes and find a mirror of her own conflict. She didn't want to be drawn to him. She wouldn't give in to the needs or emotions that were threatening her peace. She didn't trust Michael. "You can't carry me," she said, forcing the words out. The sound of her voice startled her. The husky tone was more an invitation than a protest.

"I already am." He turned to the right, making a guess as to the direction.

She cleared her throat and tried again. "How am I going to explain to..." She got no farther. Tilly came out of the kitchen, stopped and stared at Michael holding Ginger.

Michael stared back.

"I suppose you have a reason for carrying her. She doesn't look hurt as far as I can see. And it's a little early in the morning for romping about."

Amazed at Tilly's attitude, Ginger gaped. She could feel a blush starting at her hairline and heading for her toes. Michael grinned, suddenly liking the stern-faced woman.

"Actually, I'm doing a Rhett Butler imitation."

"You need the stairway for that," she pointed out, watching him. "And she's no Scarlett."

"I don't know about that. I can see some similarities." He glanced down at Ginger, the sparkle in her eyes warning of retribution to come. He welcomed the prospect, but he couldn't have explained why if asked.

"Are you eating with her?"

"I don't know. Am I?" he queried, without taking his eyes from Ginger's face.

"That depends," Ginger said, deciding it was time to enter the conversation. She would have a word with Tilly later over her unprecedented behavior.

"On what?" One dark brow lifted curiously. He rather liked carrying her, he realized. If this was being romantic, he rather liked that, too. Of course, kissing her was better, and touching her velvety skin the next step to heaven, but he was a realist. He'd take what he could get.

Ginger found herself forgetting Tilly and the reasons she shouldn't trust his gentleness or the admiring look in his eyes. She didn't want to move. All she wanted was to lay her head on his shoulder and let him hold her as he had before. The need was new and undeniable. But she fought it anyway, for she had learned the heartbreak of caring for those who put money before people.

"On your behavior."

For a moment there had been a softness about her that he couldn't resist. Then it was gone, chased away by dark memories. He wanted to ask what haunted her but knew he had no right. Not yet. His lips twisted at the irony of the fickle hand of fate. He had come to the South seeking new professional ground to build his dream on. Instead he had found something that could very well bring him to his knees. In two days, Elizabeth "Ginger" Bellwood had triggered more emotions than he had experienced in years. She made him forget business when it had been the guiding light of his climb out of the pit of poverty. Poverty had taken his childhood, and had denied him the dreams that many took for granted. He was truly a self-made man, far rougher than most of those he dealt with. The heritage that had bred Ginger was what he had strived for all his life.

"If I promise to be good?"

Ginger read the hunger about him, which had nothing to do with food. There was desire in his eyes. Wary and uneasy, she looked closer but could only see herself reflected in the pale mirrors of his eyes. "All right, but put me down."

Reluctantly, he lowered his arms, allowing her to slide slowly down his body. Tilly had retreated to the kitchen for another place setting. He only had a moment and he needed her. His head bent, his lips teasing hers as her body was teasing him with its touch.

"Don't," she whispered. Everywhere he touched her was on fire with wanting. She had never reacted so strongly to a man. The excitement of his caress blotted out all logic.

"Yes," he murmured, recognizing the lie, for her hands were pulling him closer—even as her mouth formed the denial. Despite the urgent craving of his senses, Michael touched her lips lightly, tasting rather than taking. He wanted her to want him with the same fiery need that was his pain. His lips nipped at hers, teasing the full lower one until she opened her mouth to him.

Ginger flexed her fingers on his shirt, leaning into the caress, feeling his warmth surround her. His muscles rippled in pleasure as he pressed nearer. She was crazy. The last thing she should be doing was letting him hold her and yet she couldn't help wanting him. "We shouldn't," she whispered huskily.

"I know, but I don't want to stop." His tongue slipped into her mouth, stealing the words that would deny them both.

Ginger met his hunger with equal force, straining to hold him tighter. Nothing mattered but the touch of his hands and his lips. When he lifted his head, she was breathing heavily, her breasts crushed against his chest, her hips cradling him as though they belonged together.

"Honey, you're lethal," Michael said hoarsely, knowing now he had made a mistake. The desire had not abated, only escalated to an uncomfortable degree.

Ginger was more than a stimulant to his libido. She was a danger to his self-image. He should have been pulling back, reassessing the power she seemed to have over him. Instead, he wanted to move closer to her warmth, to the vibrancy of her personality. He didn't understand her or her background. The epitome of all he had been striving to attain for himself now lay in his arms, offering herself as surely as the sun gave up its light to the darkness. Suddenly, he considered the future in a way that had nothing to do with business. It was time he thought of making a home, of having children to benefit from the empire he was building. Who better than a woman like Ginger to fill the empty place at his side?

Ginger watched the expression on his face change. She wondered at the sudden cool calculation in his eyes. Reality came crashing down, reminding her of what she had allowed to happen. Angered more at herself than at him, she pushed herself out of his arms. She reminded herself bitterly that she was not a foolish girl with stars in her eyes.

Michael frowned at her withdrawal. "What's wrong?"

"Nothing," she denied immediately, torn between embarrassment at her loss of control and the unfulfilled desire clawing at her body.

"Something is. Are you regretting—"

"Yes," she replied before he could finish. "I don't know you. And, in spite of appearances to the contrary, I don't respond this way to every personable man who crosses my path."

The lines between his brows deepened, as the thought of her with another man penetrated. He didn't want to think that she might have known or cared for someone else. Confused at the possessive thought, he reached for her. She slipped away, putting the table between them.

"What do you want from me?" She needed answers, something to hang on to, something to fight.

He shook his head to clear it. Those eyes demanded answers he couldn't give, either to her or himself. "I want to know you better." That much was true. "I want to understand why I want you. Like you, I don't come on to every passable woman I meet. For one thing, I'm too busy; and for the most part, I'm not interested enough."

Tilly entered the room, then stopped on seeing them facing off. "Not before breakfast," she said sternly.

"Whatever argument you two are starting, eat first—then fight."

"There won't be any fight," Ginger announced curtly, taking her seat. "Michael is going right after breakfast."

"Elizabeth Lenore Bellwood!" Tilly stared at her, clearly shocked by the ungracious comment.

"I could leave before."

Ginger looked at him, caught between Tilly's displeasure with her behavior and Michael's grim expression. Her headache returned in force. "Oh, sit down. You're giving me a crick in my neck to go with this blasted migraine."

Tilly was instantly all concern. "Why didn't you tell me that thing was still with you? You should be in bed, not down here cavorting around." Practically dropping the extra dishes in front of Michael she moved to Ginger's side. She tipped the younger woman's face up to scan it anxiously. "You look awfully pale. I'll call the doctor."

Ginger was torn between laughing and crying. First Tilly was all but throwing her at Michael, and now she was nearly telling the man to leave. If Ginger had felt better, she would have demanded an explanation of her housekeeper. "Leave it, please, Tilly. I'm all right, really."

"Don't lie to me. I may only be the housekeeper but I've raised you all these years and watched you suffer with these things. I knew you were doing too much."

Michael watched the exchange, learning in a few seconds that the bond between the two women was strong. The two had a more mother-daughter than employee-mistress relationship. Ensnared by her obvious affection for Tilly, Ginger was not only uncomfortable with Tilly's concern but apparently helpless to stop it. The women he had known tended to be so caught up in their careers that softer feelings were almost nonexistent. Ginger baffled him with her temper, her corporate raider business instincts and now her caring for the woman who was officially her housekeeper.

Impulsively, he interrupted, "One of the reasons I came by today was to entice Ginger out with me for a drive. That was before I knew she wasn't feeling well, of course."

Tilly aimed a glare in his direction. "Anyone can see the last thing she needs is to be racketing about the countryside in the sunlight. The light makes the pain worse," she added in a voice that openly doubted his good intentions, his sanity and his intelligence.

Ginger felt the soft chains of love dragging her up to her bed for a day of unrelenting coddling. The prospect held all the pleasure of a case of poison ivy. "I've already said I'd go. I'll wear my darkest sunglasses and put on a hat."

"You can't be serious." Tilly glared at them both.

"I won't let her overdo," Michael inserted, ignoring Ginger's indignant look.

Tilly glanced at Ginger's set face, then back at Michael. "You promise?" she demanded suspiciously.

"I promise." Having thrust himself into the role of protector, he might as well go all the way and give being a peacemaker a shot.

"I don't need a keeper," Ginger muttered.

"But maybe *I* need to care for someone." Michael surprised himself as much as Ginger with the unconscious words. "It's kind of nice to be needed occasionally for something besides check-writing."

Neither noticed that Tilly had taken herself off to the kitchen for the food. Ginger stared into Michael's eyes, seeing the yearning reflected there. "Is that what your life is?"

Now that he had opened his mouth, there was no point in trying to backtrack. "More often than not. I built it that way. Now I'm not sure I haven't made a mistake." Honesty was easier than it should have been.

Tilly returned, laying the platters of eggs, bacon, grits and biscuits between them without speaking.

Ginger shouldn't have wanted to understand. She should have been beating a hasty retreat, now that he was confirming her worst fears. "Why would you do that to yourself?"

"Probing for the dark secrets of my past?" he asked, striving for lightness.

"You wanted to know me. Maybe I would like to know the man who kisses me as though he means it." Could she be wrong? she wondered, studying him intently.

"I do mean it." He reached across the table to take her hand in his. He gazed at the slender fingers lying in his palm. There was no mark of work on the smooth flesh, no calluses, no scars or dry skin, only golden velvet textures that had known the best that life had to offer.

"How can you?" she whispered, surprised by the sincerity that even she could not doubt. "We hardly know each other. I don't think you'd be comfortable here even for a short time."

Michael raised his head, reading more into her remark than the words indicated. "My house is bigger than this one, and I don't keep antiques, but I know what they are.''

Startled at his vehemence, Ginger withdrew her hand. "That's not what I meant. I was talking about small-town life. There isn't much here for a man like you. What did you think I was talking about?" She watched him closely, once again struck by something dark and painful in his eyes.

Michael shrugged, silently cursing his quick defense. It had been years since he had felt the sting of snobbery, but it seemed he had not lost his retaliatory reflexes. "I spoke without thinking."

She shook her head, knowing he lied, without knowing how she had realized it. "I know you didn't. But I don't have the right to pry, so I won't." She reached for the platter of eggs, no longer hungry but realizing she had to eat.

Michael watched her close up on him, shutting him out of her thoughts. The pain at finding himself an outsider was surprisingly strong. Wanting to stop the pain, to see her eyes light with interest, he gave her more information than he had ever given anyone. "I grew up on the streets. I dreamed about places like this, when I was too hungry to sleep and too tired to keep fighting to get out and make something of myself," he admitted abruptly.

Ginger's hand stilled, her eyes raised to his, seeing the cost to his pride in the expression on his face. In two sentences he'd uttered a summation of a struggle that had been etched in strain and sweat and dreams.

"You succeeded," she said quietly. She could barely comprehend the price he must have paid to reach the level that was apparent in his clothes, his speech and his business.

Michael had never asked for approval from anyone but himself, yet hearing Ginger express appreciation for his achievements boosted his ego. Her tentative smile was so important he was afraid to trust it. "It isn't like this."

She tipped her head, studying him curiously. "Do you want it to be?" The moments in her life when her heritage had been a burden, came back to haunt her. "There are other kinds of poverty beyond the physical."

He almost tossed the cliché of poor little rich girl between them, but the lost, hurting look in her eyes silenced him.

"I grew up knowing that nearly every child in town would have gladly been my friend simply because I was one of the Bellwood-Lynch clan. College was no better. Even though there might have been the children of wealthier people there, few had the clout my family has in this state. I dated men who wanted a piece of the power they thought I had. My own father thought I'd make a good showing in the marriage-merger stakes. I can't think how many times I escaped being either a trophy or a boardroom casualty."

Mentally, Michael winced at the brutal and insightful analysis. If she was telling the truth, then she had known suffering, too. "They might have also been attracted to you as a person," he pointed out carefully.

"But it was the family name and power base that was the beginning." She laughed a little shakily, suddenly wishing she had not opened her mind and heart so quickly. There were dark areas in Michael that worried her. Parts of him reminded her so strongly of her father that she couldn't fully trust him not to seize on a weakness and use it to his advantage.

Feeling awkward was not her best guise, Ginger decided, shrugging uncomfortably. "How did we get on this subject? Neither of us has very good memories of our growing-up years. Let's leave it at that."

"You can't pretend our pasts aren't with us," he argued, disturbed at her need to draw back. He was no more pleased with the course of the conversation than she, but he needed to understand her.

Ginger looked away, fighting the urge to continue. He wanted too much, too fast, she reminded herself. "I'm postponing it."

He jumped on the explanation. "Until when?"

She glanced back at him, surprised at the swift demand. Uneasy, wanting to believe the desire in his eyes, remembering too many hard lessons to allow herself to be that foolish, she evaded, "I don't know."

Tilly chose that moment to come back into the dining room, bearing a fresh pot of coffee. "You two better get started on those eggs before they get cold." She refilled both cups and then departed without waiting for an answer.

Ginger picked up her fork and began eating. Michael watched her for a minute before following suit. Not having much experience in opening himself up to someone, he didn't know how to continue. He would wait and watch for an opportunity to touch her again, to reach beyond the distrust she showed so clearly to the woman who hid beneath the polite mask.

Breakfast was spent largely in silence. Neither Ginger nor Michael felt ready to speak. When the phone rang in the kitchen, it was easily heard. Tilly poked her head around the door.

"It's your assistant. He wants to speak to you immediately." Frowning, Michael rose and started for the connecting door. "You might want to use the phone in the room across the hall."

"This one is closer." More concerned with the reason that Charles had called than the etiquette of the situation, he ignored Tilly's surprised look as he passed her.

"What is it?" he demanded the moment he lifted the receiver.

"You aren't going to like it," Charles said with a sigh.

"There hasn't been much I have liked since I arrived in this town," he returned bluntly.

"There's been a fire in your room."

Michael's jaw clenched. "How did it start and how much damage did the fire do?"

"The faulty wiring in the air conditioner. What the smoke didn't get, the volunteer fire department did."

"Have I got any clothes left?"

"Not any that wouldn't qualify as dust rags. Your briefcase is a total write-off."

"And the papers in it." He raked his fingers through his hair, wondering if there was such a thing as a Lynch Creek jinx. "Get on the phone to the office and get my secretary to go to the house for a replacement wardrobe. Have a duplicate set of papers sent down and find us another place to stay. If one air conditioner caused this, there's no telling what else lies in store for us in that place."

The silence that greeted his orders was uncharacteristic. "Now what?" Michael demanded, knowing he wasn't going to like whatever Charles had to say.

"There isn't anything closer than Brunswick. I've already checked."

"That's an hour's drive."

"One way," Charles said gloomily.

"Ideas?" Michael asked.

"Not one."

Ginger stood in the doorway, having heard the conversation. At the mention of fire she had been unable to keep up the pretense that she wasn't listening. "I have one," she offered, on impulse. The moment the words were out, she wondered if her headache had temporarily disrupted her intelligence. For all that she was attracted to Michael, there was still the property dispute between them.

Michael turned to find her watching him with sympathy in her eyes. Surprisingly, he felt some of his anger die. "What?"

"You and your assistant can stay here. There's plenty of room." Two days ago, she wouldn't have thought of making the suggestion. Now it seemed right. She smiled hesitantly, not certain how she would feel if he rejected her help.

Part of him said it was only good business to be in town. It was too bad that wasn't his only motivation, he added silently. "Are you sure?"

"Yes." Her smile widened to a more natural curve. His was slow in coming but it did appear.

"Charles, pack your stuff up and get over to Bellwood Ridge. A very nice lady by the name of Tilly will let you in if I'm not here. Elizabeth has offered us shelter and a place at the table." He hung up on Charles's grunt of surprise and approval. Walking toward Ginger, he tried to remember that Tilly was hovering in the background watching them. He wanted to pull Ginger into his arms but contented himself with tucking her hand in the crook of his arm. Her smile, and the look in her eyes, was more than a reward for his restraint. For the moment the mistrust that she seemed to feel for him was in hiding. Her glance showed her pleasure at his acceptance of her suggestion. Oddly, he felt ten feet tall and able to leap tall buildings on demand.

"Honey, you have a way of making the sun shine brighter," he murmured as he seated her at the table again.

Five

The sun was shining, bathing the landscape in gold. The breeze from the open car window brought in the scent of flowers and pine. Ginger sat back, thinking over the last two hours. The migraine finally releasing its grip on her had a lot to answer for. She had made some major mistakes in her dealings with Michael. For one, she had offered him a place in her home. Bellwood Ridge was the computerized nerve center of Bellwood-Lynch Enterprises and paradoxically, the one haven she had from those who would impose their demands on her. Now she had willfully brought Michael and the conflicting feelings that he aroused in her into her sanctuary. On top of that, there was still the property issue. Until that was resolved, she had to remember his reputation for succeeding where others failed. Although honest by reputation, he turned over every stone to achieve an advantage when he was confronted with a problem. She didn't want the attraction between them to become a stone that would bruise her heart. Acknowledging her fear, Ginger tucked her emotions away. Until she was certain of her ground, she would deal with Michael Sheridan in the only way she thought he would understand. She disliked business games, but she played them well. She'd learned at her father's knee just how to survive in the *real* world.

But first she would finish one of the personal issues that lay between them. "Thank you for getting me out of the house."

Michael smiled at her. He could feel himself relaxing. The silence that had fallen between them was a comfortable one. For the first time, he began to appreciate the slower pace of Ginger's world. It had been many years since he had taken time to slow down. "I had a feeling you'd be climbing out the window if someone didn't cut you loose."

"Probably, and then I never would've heard the end of it. There is an oak tree with a very strategically placed branch next to my balcony. It wouldn't be the first time I've used that exit."

Startled, Michael did a double take. He couldn't imagine Ginger doing anything so out of keeping with her upbringing. "I was only teasing."

"I wasn't."

He thought that over. Perhaps there was more to this woman than he had discovered. Intrigued, when he would rather have been put off, he asked, "What else do you do?"

"That's a loaded question if I ever heard one."

"You know what I mean," he replied impatiently, hearing something in her voice which had not been there before. A kind of coolness enfolded her words. He wanted her smile and instead received a clear-eyed look that was disturbing. On his guard, he tried to fathom the change even as he spoke. "Grown women do not climb trees."

"I don't know. I imagine some do. Just because we get older, doesn't mean we have to give up all the fun things."

"Like walking down the main street of town eating ice cream cones." Surely those lips would curve now.

"Why not? What's the harm?"

"My suit, for one." To his disappointment, no humor sparkled in her eyes.

"I wonder why it doesn't seem to occur to us wise grown-ups that young children, before adults can teach them otherwise, have the right of the world? They trust because they haven't been taught fear. They tell the truth because they haven't learned the dubious value of a lie. They enjoy the moment with all that is in them. They don't consider what someone else might think when they decide to do something. And most of all, they forgive and love you, if you give them even half a chance. They might react out of temper and hurt a playmate's feelings, but they are just as quick to apologize and make amends with the offer of sharing some treasure. Their needs are immediate, simple and, for them, the most important thing in their lives at a given moment. Adults don't have that intensity for life, for the most part, nor do they have the ability to believe that anything is possible."

Michael was silenced by her disturbing words. In an offbeat way they made sense. His own deprived childhood notwithstanding, he could understand what she meant. "They also don't get ulcers, heart attacks and stress burnout."

Her faint smile held sadness and acceptance, although she said nothing.

"You can't live in this world with those kinds of reactions," he added.

"I think you can. I refuse to spend my life tied, hand and toe, by a bunch of sophisticated rules that do nothing but make me miserable. If I let it, Bellwood-Lynch would take over my life. When I wanted to move my headquarters to the Ridge, my advisers said it couldn't be done. They were wrong about that, and quite a few other things, as well. For the most part, corporate games turn my stomach, but I do know the rules and I also bend them. I believe in honesty and redress of mistakes rather than covering up as much as possible. When I give my word I keep it, and I expect others to do the same. That's why I'm even considering selling off any part of Bellwood land."

"With a few conditions," he couldn't help pointing out, curious to see how she would explain away her stipulations.

She shrugged, undisturbed by the faint mockery in his words. "Your company intends to become part of the town and ultimately use the facilities. Your contribution is a fair exchange. For you it's a goodwill gesture that won't hurt your cause."

Michael glanced at her sharply. "So you know the town isn't completely in favor of Sheridan Electronics moving here?"

"I've had to fight my own battles with some of the citizens' shortsightedness. Besides, there's nothing that goes on in this area that I don't know about." It was a simple statement of fact, not one born of arrogance or conceit. "I suspect part of the reason that you came to see me this morning is because you're aware that you can't afford enemies. Your assistant was in the barbershop yesterday."

She turned, looking at him, searching for truth in the eyes of a master player. Her team of researchers had been most explicit in the investigation she had requested yesterday. They had had a report, received via computer, on her desk by the time she had returned from Brunswick. She hadn't lied when she had said her business was conducted with honesty and straight-line tactics. But she'd left out telling him about her careful use of dossiers describing those she dealt with. When you ate with the devil, you had to be sure that he didn't hide a tiger under the table.

"So?"

"He was asking questions of the local gossip mill, during the time you were ranting and raving at me on the phone."

His temper rippled beneath the surface of his calm expression. Few people had the courage to speak to him in this fashion. That she would didn't surprise him as much as it should have. He was beginning to understand her. "I *do not* rant or rave."

"You can call it what you want, but you lost your temper. Not a good move, by the way. Then you talked to your assistant and discovered something your people should have already considered and made allowances for. At a guess, I'd bet you were furious. Eating crow, no matter how it's cooked, wouldn't sit well with a success-oriented man like yourself."

By the time she reached the last statement, Michael was beyond being angry. He was fascinated at her cool analysis and the way she seemed to accept his reason-

ing without emotion. He had met the woman named
Ginger, but now he was going toe-to-toe with the
business person who guided Bellwood-Lynch Enterprises through the corporate maze. The change was
startling and impressive. Her voice was smooth, with
no hint of the usual soft accent. Her face was calm—
not expressionless, simply calm. She spoke with pre-
cision, cutting through to the heart of the matter with
the skill of a master surgeon. Respect for more than
the woman was born in that moment. Also, oddly, he
found himself devoutly glad she seemed to be on his
side.

"That's a fairly harsh judgment of my motives for
seeking you out."

"Accurate," she corrected. "Predictable. The only
question remaining, is whether we'll do business." She
gestured toward the dirt road ahead on the right. "We
turn here."

Michael made the turn, then glanced at her curiously. "I might have had other reasons for coming to
see you," he murmured, wondering if her composure
was a pose or a reality.

"Our 'chemistry,' for want of a better word?"

He had his answer in the cool way she met his eyes.
"I can think of prettier phrases." If he had not felt her
melt in his arms, if he had not known the heat of passion in her kiss, he would have thought himself talking to a woman who had not known the touch of
desire.

Her brows arched in surprise, a slight smile curved
her lips. "The last thing I would have expected out of
you is a need for flowery words. You deal in profit and
loss. The bottom-line mentality." She pointed to a
large tree beside the road. "Pull over. We're here."

Michael did as she directed without debating her assessment of his character. The truth was, he didn't have a defense. But what bothered him was the feeling that he wished he did.

Ginger could see the confusion in his face. She should have felt satisfaction that her tactics were working, but all she knew was a sense of loss. She wanted to trust him and herself. She preferred the desire in his eyes to that searching look that probed her mind, calculated the odds of success and looked for an opening to win the battle. Sighing deeply, she got out of the car, telling herself she should have learned the futility of looking for the moon in a hole dug all the way to China. Michael's personality had been formed for a long time—just as hers had been. He saw her life as easy. She knew the truth. Neither of them had had much of a chance to grow into adulthood without receiving a full complement of scars and defenses. Desire had made them both vulnerable. Right now he was in the mood to try to understand but would he always be?

"This is it?" Michael demanded, staring at the rolling hills in disbelief. "Why didn't you tell me that the topography was so much more rugged than the piece you took?"

"It's cleared."

"Big deal. You know that most of this will have to be leveled. That means big earth movers, lost time, man-hours."

"It depends on how you do the job. If you pushed it you could get it done in about ninety days."

"Working round the clock, maybe," he agreed irritably. "Just look at those hills. There isn't a flat place on the whole three hundred acres that is big enough to put up a one-family residence, much less a factory or the parking lots.''

''Do you want it or not?'' She leaned against the car, watching him as he glanced at the land.

''What choice do I have unless I'm willing to scrap the whole project?''

Ginger said nothing.

Michael turned away from the site to look at Ginger. ''All right.'' There was nothing in her face to indicate her opinion of his decision. He wasn't sure whether he was glad or sorry that she offered him no opportunity to relieve his frustration.

''I have the papers ready at home. You can look them over this weekend or send them to your lawyers.'' She turned, intending to get into the car.

Michael caught her arm, pulling her around to face him. ''You have the papers ready?'' he demanded angrily, now having a target for his emotions. No one, since he had learned the rules of the world he had chosen as his arena, had ever beaten him so completely. Not only had she snatched his property from beneath his nose, but she had learned enough about him to predict his reactions.

''It was the only logical step for you to take.''

Even now the voice was calm, without inflection. He searched her eyes, looking for the woman, needing an outlet. ''Is this logical?'' he asked, giving in to the need to pull her into his arms and stamp his mark on her. Primitive emotions had never been his driving force, but since meeting Ginger he had discovered caveman tendencies were a fact of his life. His lips took hers, his hands molding her to his body, imprinting her flesh with his scent and his strength.

Ginger pushed against his chest, fighting him as she had not done in the past. She understood the look on his face too well. Angry, she wedged her arms between their bodies as she closed her lips tight against him.

"Damn you," she breathed harshly when he tried to pull her closer. His eyes glittered with rage as he stared at her.

"I could say the same."

She faced him, unintimidated by the irate look. Bowing to a man, any man, was not her style. "What have I done? You made the rules. I played by them. Don't change them now. Or do you think that overpowering me physically will make you feel better?"

The scathing contempt in her voice cut through his temper. Disgust flickered, then grew stronger, as the realization of what he had tried to do shot through him. He jerked his hands away from her body, as though she were suddenly white-hot.

She stepped back slowly, not one hint of fear on her face.

"I wouldn't have forced you," he admitted in a quieter tone.

She could hurt him now. She knew it, as surely as she knew the sun would kiss the night hello. "I know."

His head lifted higher, his eyes searching for sarcasm and finding only truth.

She answered the question he did not ask. "You hold yourself in. I pushed you. You exploded. In a way, our worlds collided." She looked away from his face for a moment, gathering strength. "It was as much my fault as yours. I don't trust you. There are too many reasons why I don't trust what you make me feel. I have my defenses, too."

He studied her, hearing in her voice the sign of weakness that he could have used against her. He stepped closer, needing to hear what she had to say, more than he needed or wanted a weapon. "Why don't you trust me?"

She looked at him then, her eyes bright with tears. "I have some land you want. You could be out for gain or for revenge. Those are two very good reasons why you could pretend to want me. I know I'm not bad looking. You respond to me. I respond to you. Emotions can be counterfeited, if the reason is strong enough, or someone can be fooled into thinking a lie is a truth. I don't know which it is with us."

Her words were a mirror of his own confusion. Her pain was no less real than his own, and that surprised him. "I didn't come down here to find a woman. I wouldn't try to make love to you for some sort of social achievement or to retaliate for the loss of the land. I don't work that way." He risked raising his hand to her cheek, feeling immeasurably relieved when she didn't reject his touch. "I don't lie in my personal life, and I lie rarely doing business. I may not have your black-and-white approach to the world, but I do believe in honesty. I want you. No reason, no revenge, no gain. Need, pure and simple."

She shook her head before he finished speaking. "Neither of us is that naive. There's nothing simple between us. What would you see for us down the line if we had a relationship?"

He stepped closer, his body brushing hers. His hand slid down her throat, to settle just above the sweet curve of her breast. "I see a challenge for both of us. As you pointed out, we have a number of reasons for not trusting ourselves. But you are forgetting the people we are. Neither of us has had it easy. Taking over for your father when you were twenty-four was no one's idea of a picnic. Our rules aren't the same, but we do have one thing in common. We like beating the odds and winning. I'm offering you a chance to match me. Give me a chance to match you. The rules of the game are total honesty and as much pleasure as either of us can handle."

"You're crazy." She moved closer, his words enticing her, when she would rather have been able to turn away. The tree shielded them from sight from the road on one side and the car screened them on the other.

"Determined." His free hand curled around her waist as his fingers cupped her breast.

She leaned into the caress, her lips parting. "We could get hurt."

"I know." His fingers teased the nipple into a hard peak. "In that, we start even."

"What about trust?" Her hands slid under his pullover shirt to the smooth flesh beneath.

"We'll learn as we go along. I'm no better at that than you seem to be." He tipped his hips against hers, slowly rotating his body to pleasure them both.

"And if we don't?" She pushed his shirt up, wanting one less layer of material separating them.

"Then we both lose." He unbuttoned her shirt, parting the fabric to bare her breasts. "And we know we'd hate that."

Ginger gasped when he brought her nipples in contact with the soft mat of hair on his chest. The rough feel of the strands pulling lightly across the peaks sent darts of fire through her. Her legs trembled with the force of the desire his touch created.

"Can you really deny this?" he demanded, watching her body react to his even as he felt the pain of his own arousal.

Her eyes met his, seeing he was as vulnerable as she. "No, but I think we're both crazy to try," she whispered before slipping her arm around his neck to draw his head down. Her mouth took his, needing his kiss to seal the all-or-nothing game between them.

Michael took all she offered, drinking from her lips with a desperate hunger he had never before known. In the full light of day, on a deserted road, he forgot every goal he had set for himself, every promise he had made, except for the two he had given the woman he held in his arms. His world narrowed, defining itself in the moan on her lips and the arching body that struggled for a completion of the union of their flesh.

"I want to make love to you here."

"We can't," she breathed, regret deepening her voice to a hoarse whisper.

"Then find us a place. I can't take you home." He lifted her in his arms, carrying her to the car.

Ginger was lost, unable to think of one place private enough that half the town wouldn't find out about it. Frustration cut through the fog of sensuality. She blinked, sitting up as he edged into the car on the passenger side, his arms drawing her close. "Wait," she said, suddenly remembering it was her car they had, not his rental one.

"Don't tell me there isn't a spot. I don't care how far we have to go." Desire roughened his voice.

"I have it." She leaned into him, silencing him with her lips, when he would have asked questions. Her tongue found a ready mate in his. For a moment she gave in to the need of her body, taking his mouth with all the urgency that drove her. "Trust me to get us there," she pleaded, when she raised her head.

Their eyes met, each knowing the other was accustomed to the ordering of his own life. To put themselves into each other's hands was new, carrying more than a hint of danger. "Is your headache gone?" His fingers shook slightly as he brushed her temples.

"What little is left doesn't matter."

"Are you sure?"

Neither pretended he was asking about her physical well-being, with the second question. "Yes."

"All right."

Ginger started the car without a word, guiding it back the way they had come. The silence was not easy between them. Doubts filled her mind and she knew Michael had to have his own second thoughts. She didn't like needing him so much that she was willing to go to him without complete trust. To her, risks were a fact of life, but she had never taken one as great as this. In the past there had always been some kind of safety net. With Michael there was no parachute. She was taking a blind leap into the future.

Michael stared at the road which was growing progressively less civilized by the minute. Bumps became teeth-rattling potholes. He glanced at Ginger, watching as she concentrated on the dirt cow path twisting before them. He wanted to ask where they were going, but didn't. She had asked for his trust. For this, he could give it.

"Damn!" he swore, caught unaware by a jolt that knocked his head into the car ceiling.

Ginger shot him a quick look, her apology swift but distracted. "Hold on. It's going to get worse before it gets better."

"I had a dentist at one of those indigent care centers tell me that once. I was seven at the time. I bit him before *better* ever rolled around," he muttered in satisfaction, rubbing the top of his head as he glared at the road.

Ginger laughed, surprised at his dry wit. Nothing that had passed between them had indicated his ability to appreciate the humor in life. "Close your eyes," she demanded.

Michael stared at her as if she had taken leave of her sanity. "Is this some kind of test?"

"No. I want you to be surprised."

She was serious, he realized. He looked around the dense underbrush that surrounded them. He could see nothing that warranted a second glance. He could feel her waiting for his decision. Oddly, he felt as if more rode on his response than the request suggested.

"Do you know, I don't think there is one other person that I would do this for," he said, sighing in resignation. His lashes drifted shut. "In fact, I'm sure of it. I feel like a fool, sitting here in the dark, while you send us down this godforsaken road again. A man could get severely injured this way."

Ginger knew she would never forget this moment as long as she lived. Michael's body was tight with tension, but his eyes were closed as she eased the car forward. She couldn't have said what had prompted her to use the childish phrase on him. She had been as startled as he, when he complied with her command.

Suddenly the scruffy foliage gave way to a small lake nestled in the tiny valley created by three hills. Trees that stretched to the water's edge rimmed the fourth side, for the moment shielding a beaver dam from view. Beyond the trees was a patch of clover as soft as the down comforter on her bed. The pines acted as a canopy, shutting out the sun. No one, as far as Ginger knew, had discovered this spot, located right in the heart of the first holdings of Bellwood Ridge.

"You can look now," she whispered, her eyes on his face, rather than on the primitive paradise that she had brought him to share.

Michael studied the scene. It looked so perfect that it could have been a rural painting. "Where are we?"

"Where it all began for my family. See that chimney over there. The first Bellwood home was built on that spot. The cabin was so small it would have fit into the entrance hall at the Ridge. I grew up with Tilly telling me about my great-great-granddaddy and his wife, Mattie."

"I'm surprised your father didn't do the honors, instead of Tilly. I understand he was quite proud of his heritage?"

It took a second for her to realize he must have been really checking out her family to know of Lyle's exorbitant pride in his name. "He told me nothing," she said flatly. The last person she wanted to discuss was her sire. She turned away from Michael's curious eyes to reach in the back for the quilt she always kept on hand. She saw Michael reach out to her, but she evaded him by getting out of the car. "Have you changed your mind?"

Michael joined her but made no attempt to touch her. "What have I said?"

Ginger started to say nothing, then remembered her promise. "I don't talk about him to anyone," she admitted, the words drawn from her.

He saw the pain and the pride in her expression. The dignity that held a wealth of emotions he could barely decipher. He wanted to fold her into his arms and promise her that whatever had put that look on her face would never touch her again. But equally, he wanted to pull away from the feelings that were tying him to her. Desire was an emotion he could handle. The conditions for their coming together were taking tolls he had not thought to pay. Platitudes filled his mind, empty words, white lies that he almost spoke but didn't because of the pact they had made.

"This isn't easy, being honest."

"I know." She turned her head away, needing a moment to compose herself. "Maybe I shouldn't have brought you here. This is a special place for me. I don't think anyone even remembers it exists anymore."

"Do you want to leave?" He watched her, not sure which answer he preferred.

"Do you?" she asked without turning her head.

He hesitated, then said slowly, "No, but I'm not sure I'm ready to make love now."

She looked at him then, the tension in her face slowly easing. "It's quiet here, peaceful. I lie on the quilt some days and just let things be."

He sighed deeply, feeling his body relax. "I haven't just stopped in a very long time. I think I would like to now." Without thinking, he held out his hand. She glanced at it and so did he. Strange, but he had never offered to hold a woman's hand before.

Ginger placed her fingers in his, liking the way his warmth wrapped around her. "Do you have to be anywhere?"

He shook his head, wondering what else in his life was missing. Ginger was teaching him things he had not known he needed to learn. "But if I did, I think I would cancel them."

Her smile touched him. The sun shone and he noticed it for the first time in many years.

Six

Michael spread the multicolored quilt in a patch of shade, watching his actions as though he were outside himself. After the deprivation of his early life, he was no enthusiast for the more primitive forms of relaxation. His idea of a good time was a French restaurant, a superb bottle of wine, a sophisticated woman on his arm and a bed with silk sheets at the end of the evening.

Ginger sat down on the quilt, drawing her knees up to her chin. She stared out at the lake, searching for the peace that usually surrounded her in this place.

"Do you like picnics?" Michael asked abruptly.

"Yes." She glanced at him to find him studying her as though he were attempting to fathom some mystery. "Why?"

"I don't. Not that I've been on that many."

"Does that have something to do with us?"

He ignored the question, intent on understanding. "How about backpacking?"

His queries were disturbing, but she couldn't figure out why. "I haven't done that, but I do ride horses. That's how I found this place."

He didn't look around. "I don't know how to ride."

"I could teach you if you wanted to learn." The offer was out before she realized it.

Michael shook his head, his mind immediately conjuring up all manner of things they could do together, none of which was possible in public. "I'd waste both our time. There isn't any place to keep a horse where I live, even if I had the inclination."

"And you don't have the inclination," she finished for him, frowning. "What *do* you do for relaxation?"

"A good restaurant. A play." He shrugged, leaving out the companionship he sometimes sought. "I don't have that much time for the most part. The days are rarely long enough for all I want to get done as it is."

She understood overloaded schedules, but she also knew the value of periodic breaks. "But you've made it. You don't have to keep pushing."

His glance was sharp, shrewd. "You're not naive."

"No, but I know no one has to keep going on after a certain point unless all you're after is more money."

If someone else had probed, he would have turned the questions aside. But for now, with Ginger, he found he could answer. "It was never that." He slipped his arm around her waist and pulled her close. The smell of flowers in the air wasn't nearly as sweet as her scent. "I started out just making sure I would never know cold or hunger again. Then I discovered I needed to insure the small place I had made for myself. In my world there is always someone bigger and meaner just around the corner. My tastes changed with each rung on the ladder. The challenge got to me. I rose higher." He was explaining to her and himself, another first in his life. And it, too, was right.

"The carousel started spinning, and now you don't know how to get off," she said, as she leaned against him.

"I don't know that I want to get off," he corrected, looking at her without attempting to soften his words. "I don't know that I could do what you have done. You like this small-town pace and tolerate the big-city games. With me, it's the other way around."

It took a moment to understand the frustration she heard in his voice. "Perhaps it will never matter that our worlds are so far apart."

"And perhaps it will." He hadn't meant to put his concern into words, hadn't even been sure he had the words to make himself clear.

Ginger searched his face uncertainly, feeling as bewildered by what was happening to them as she guessed he was. "Do you want to forget the game?"

He sighed deeply, remembering his promise of honesty. "When I hold you close, it's easy to say no."

She nodded. That, she could understand. "It's the same for me."

"This honesty stuff is tough." He touched her face, tracing the delicate bones that gave her face the elegance of pure breeding. "We're so different. I can put on an expensive suit, custom-made shoes. I can speak as though I have a college education—but I don't."

"Do you think I care?" The idea was appalling.

"If you don't, you should," he stated flatly.

Her hands encircled his wrists. "You aren't a fool, so don't talk like one. I know quite a few college graduates who couldn't find their way out of a grocery store without a road map printed in first-grade words." Being vulnerable to each other was one thing. Being vulnerable to the prejudices of the world was unacceptable. "My father had a masters degree in business, and he couldn't have done what you did. He might have led a street gang, but he wouldn't have taken a dream and made it into a reality."

Her eyes were alive with truth, sincerity and, he would have bet his life, belief in him. No one had ever believed in him before. "You can't know I did that."

"Bet?" She shook the arms she held. "I have a file on you put together by the company's research team. What they didn't find out wasn't worth the time of looking. I even know that you prefer blondes to brunettes and that you've never dated a redhead in your life. I can tell you the color of the towels in your bathroom and what you had for lunch the day you left Baltimore. And if I had been interested, I probably could have found out every secret that you had."

Startled that she would admit to an investigation, he murmured, "Sounds like your people are better than mine. They had next to nothing on you. Of course, I didn't know the part you would play in the sale, and they had to do a hurry-up job when I did find out." He wrapped his fingers around the back of her neck, while his thumbs lightly stroked the curve of her lips. "I don't think I like you knowing so much about me."

"Call your people and have them check on me further. Better yet, ask what you want. I gave you my word on honesty. I won't take it back." The offer was an impulse she didn't regret making.

"Do you have a lover?"

The question hit hard, coming so swiftly Ginger had no way to prepare herself. Her eyes darkened with pain. "Do you really think I would be with you like this if I had?"

"No. I believed you when you spoke of honesty and nothing I've learned of you since has changed my mind."

"Then that's your answer. Now your turn."

"I don't either, but my file should have told you that."

"It would have, but I didn't read that part. It had nothing to do with what I thought would occur between us," she added on seeing his surprise. "Clearly a miscalculation on my part."

Whether Ginger meant it or not, her words were a challenge tossed between them. Michael's head lifted, all thoughts focused on her, not trying to understand or to probe but simply to be with her. She was part witch, part woman he decided as he watched the stray shafts of sun tease her lips with every movement. He liked sitting in the shade with no one to hear them but the creatures of the woods. He liked testing her mind, sharing thoughts with her that he had given to no other, while her skin rippled and flowed beneath his fingers. Bending his head, his lips brushed hers. But he wanted more. "Kiss me. Let's have done with talking for a while."

Ginger sucked in her breath as his mouth played tag with hers. The questions that still lay between them were forgotten as the magic of his touch took over. He nipped gently, then retreated. She sought to catch him, but he only allowed her a taste before sliding away to tease her ears, the sensitive spot near her temple, her eyelids. Her hands came up to capture his head. "This wasn't in our agreement," she breathed as she pulled him closer. Her mouth took the words he would have spoken but still he eluded her. His tongue darted in and slipped away before she could satisfy the steadily building hunger. Heat flowed in her body, the need to press her flesh to his touching her with urgency. She arched, her nails flexing.

"Careful, woman," he warned.

"Play fair," she whispered back.

"Make me." She was catching fire in his arms, and he could feel the need to hold the flames until they burned out of control growing within him. He wanted her out of control. He wanted to be out of control himself.

Ginger moaned deep in her throat, his challenge acting as a match to dry tinder. Her hands slipped beneath his shirt, dragging it over his head. "I'm not like this," she said huskily, even as her fingers reached for him, teasing the male nipples until they were rock-hard.

"I'm glad. I don't want anyone to know you this way," he breathed, unbuttoning her blouse and pulling it from her body. Her breasts strained toward him, the peaks blushing deep rose. There was nothing about her that didn't attract him. His hands closed around the fullness, delighting in her groan of pleasure as he took the first tip into his mouth.

Ginger buried her fingers in his hair, thrusting her body high, as desire built. His muscles contracted against her, heightening the sensation of being possessed. Michael was hard, warm and demanding. She traced his back, her fingers kneading his flesh to find all the places that gave him the pleasure his touch had brought her. Her lips followed the path of her hands, copying his actions as he whispered his need to her in words that would have shocked her from anyone else.

"Yes," she pleaded when his mouth traced a path to her navel, the tip of his tongue dipping again and again into the small well. She pulled on his shoulders, demanding the union her body craved.

He raised his head, smiling at her urgency even as his own arousal reached a painful level. "Soon. Go slowly. Make it last." His hands held her, fighting her need and his own.

"No, now." Her eyes were glazed with desire, her lids heavy. She was melting and she wanted him for his strength.

He touched her, feeling the dampness between her legs, knowing that he had brought her to this fever pitch. Her moan was like music that called to him beyond the bounds of anything he had known. His fingers moved. She arched, crying out as she peaked without him. His smile widened at the power that flowed from her to him. For a moment he felt as though he could dare anything and win.

Ginger shivered as spasms of pleasure and release washed over her. She was filled, yet empty. Satisfied, yet yearning for more. Forcing her eyes open, she stared at him as he lay with his chest pressing into her womb. His hands still held her, his body still hard with his own need.

"Why?" she whispered, feeling more vulnerable than she ever had before.

"I wanted to watch you. I wanted to give you something that I had never given anyone before."

The words were simple, the look in his blazing eyes was not. "I don't understand," she whispered, very much afraid she did. A tiny flicker of trust lifted its head in her soul.

"If you turned me away right now, I would go."

Her hands lifted, tracing his face, feeling him tremble with her touch. He was completely sensitive to her, straining at the ties that held him from her. He wanted her. The look in his eyes, the hardness pressed against her leg told her that, yet still he held back—tense, waiting for something from her that she barely understood.

"I won't turn you away." Against the odds, the trust grew stronger.

"I want you to belong to me."

Caught in the merging of the past and the present, Ginger struggled for a foothold in her changing emotions. "I want no one else," she said, giving what reassurance she could. She gasped, arching as his hands moved over her again.

"For this?"

Even through the haze of passion clouding her thinking, she felt his need for reassurance. "For more."

"Be sure." His fingers flicked the heart of her desire, teasing her and himself. He was crazy to push her and deny himself, but some part of him he barely knew demanded assurances.

"I am." Ginger fought off the lassitude and reached for him. He rose over her, filling her with one stroke. "You are more than this for me. Even now I know that. Let it be enough that we are together." Her lashes lifted and she held his gaze completely as she sheathed his body. "As we are joined, so shall we stay—so long as we both wish. That is all I can give you."

Michael felt something indefinable inside of him give way. His uncertainty vanished as he took her mouth and joined himself completely to her. His need was so great, her cry of pleasure drove him over the edge of sanity. His seed spilled in a rush of passion that did not cease until she, too, joined in the mating, rushing up to meet him as she cried his name in the wilderness. He held her tight while she shivered in the aftermath, her curves slick with the dampness that came after the fire. His hands soothed her flesh as he lifted her on top of him without leaving the warm glove of her flesh that held him so tightly.

"Trusting is so hard," Ginger murmured when she could breathe evenly again. Her cheek was tucked against Michael's shoulder, so that she could hear his heart beating.

"I've learned too many lessons in too many schools." His fingers wound through the flame-colored hair. He watched the sun play hide-and-seek for the gold in the strands.

"I want nothing from you."

"We're a pair, you and I. I wish I hadn't done that. I don't play power games in bed. It isn't fair to either partner." It was odd, but he couldn't remember a time when he had apologized to anyone or a time when the need to do so had been so great.

She raised her head, her eyes searching his. "You didn't hurt me."

"Not physically."

"Not mentally, either." Her fingers outlined his lips, a smile curving her mouth when he kissed the tips. "You needed something from me that I was glad to give. I wouldn't have wished to make love with you if you believed that sex was all that we have."

"So you took from yourself to give to me?" She healed places in him he had not known hurt. Her words were soft, that slight slurring of her ancestry a delicate music that he found soothing and pleasing.

"To give to us. Ask me for more than I'm prepared to give and I'll deny you. Anger me, and I'll fight with you. Touch me, and I'll want you. Honesty." She brushed his lips, teasing the bottom one until he took her mouth in a hot kiss. "My promise, and I don't give it lightly—for I'm no better at trusting than you," she added when she lifted her head. "I brought you here to a place where I've brought no one else. In its own way, that was my test. I won't apologize for it. I needed the reassurance just as you did. I know very well this isn't your world, but if sex had been your only goal, you would have showed your need to leave this primitive setting even if you had stayed. You accepted it and gave me more pleasure than I've ever known. I don't regret what we did."

He forced himself not to show how much her words meant to him. "What comes next? I may live in a large city, but I'm not so ignorant that I don't know some of the problems of small-town life."

She sighed, seeing as he did the difficulties of a liaison between them. "Tilly won't like it, but despite appearances she doesn't rule me. I can't say that the gossip won't bother me, but it's far from the first time the town has talked about me."

Michael frowned at the acceptance in her voice. He, who rarely cared what people thought, found himself angered that she would be subjected to gossip. "For now we should be all right. Charles is at the house and everyone probably knows about the fire." Even as he spoke his mind raced with possibilities of how to protect Ginger. He could rent an apartment in King's End or Brunswick or even Macon. None were not that far away.

She smiled at him, knowing herself better than he did. "Do you think I'll be able to hide the fact that I've given myself to you? Do you think that I wish to? My family has spent its life living up to its name. My father saw nothing but the Bellwood-Lynch heritage and would have sold his soul if it had meant the difference between our survival and oblivion. I'm not like that. I believe in myself and my choices. I climb because I want to. I eat ice cream cones because they happen to be my secret passion. Nothing I do is for shock value."

"Then we could have gone back to Bellwood Ridge."

She shook her head. "No. Your position here is tenuous. By now, everyone knows that you wanted the land I bought. Sleeping with me wouldn't look good to them. Your position will barely improve if you accept the tract I offered you."

He stared at her, unable to believe that she had thought of their need for each other enough to see the danger he had not considered. That she spoke of assets and disadvantages in the way others would see his time with her disturbed him. "I don't like this," he muttered finally, his eyes blazing with more than passion.

"It's a fact of our lives."

"It sounds as though I'm using you."

"I know that you aren't."

He watched her, wanting to be certain she believed he had come because he wanted her and not for what she could mean to his dream. With another woman, it wouldn't have mattered. "How can you be sure?"

"I have to be. Just as you had to be," she whispered.

Michael looked into Ginger's eyes and saw a determination to match his own. This woman with hands so soft that they would not snag silk, with a voice that was never once raised above the most moderate of tones and with a delicately built body that he would never forget, was a woman with courage and passion. She dared to risk herself with a man she had no reason to trust. She protected him when he had not known that he needed protection. She thought of him as no one else had ever done. And she asked nothing. Stunned, puzzled, and not certain he completely believed in her strength, he pulled her close.

"I don't know how to handle you," he confessed.

"Same here." Her eyes were sad, but her smile was bright, determined to take what was offered today and deal with tomorrow when it came. "But I think I am going to enjoy trying." Her hands slipped over his chest to find him, cupping him until his arousal was warm and hard in her hand.

He lay back, giving himself into her keeping. The shadows played over her skin as she bent over him, her lips tracing patterns on his body that fed the flames. Her hair teased like tiny feathers, licking then retreating. He groaned, writhing as she built the need. Her laugh was triumphant and full of a woman's power.

"Are you a witch, woman?" he demanded, as her eyes glowed like emeralds.

"Catch me, and find out." She slid up his chest, nipping at his lips and then retreating before he could deepen the kiss. Her hips settled over his, wrapping around the shaft of life that rose to meet her.

"You play a dangerous game, Elizabeth Bellwood. Not a lady's way at all."

"I told you I please myself."

"And me." His hands cupped her breasts, his thumbs flicking the nipples into erect peaks. He ceased to try to kiss her. There were other ways to tame his woman. Her gasp brought a primitive smile to his lips. His eyes devoured the golden flesh that trembled at his touch.

Ginger arched, posing for him, delighting in the hungry look on his face. "I could stay here all day. Mistress of all I survey," she teased him huskily.

He chuckled as he rolled her over so that she was pinned beneath him. "Speak now, oh, mistress."

She laughed up at him as she tightened her muscles and felt him jump at the pleasure that streaked through him.

"Your body language is something else, Ginger spice."

He had never enjoyed foreplay so much. Her smiles were tantalizing, invitations to delight and joy. He wanted more.

"Yours is good, too," she whispered, nipping at his ear. "Do you like to skinny dip?"

"As in that lake?" he asked, more involved with her subtle actions than her words.

"Yes. Let's make love in the lake, with water all around us. It's warm, and the sun is shining."

He sucked on her breast as the picture slipped into his mind, bringing him to a new high. The image of her golden skin slick with water, the feel of her bumping against him as the extra buoyancy of the aquatic environment gave them both a freedom that they didn't have on land. He was hot already and the added incentive almost sent him over the edge. Only his willpower kept him back.

He raised his head, lifting her up at the same time. "I hope you can swim."

"Like a fish," she murmured as he cradled her in his arms and headed for the lake.

"I can't believe I'm doing this," he added as he waded into the water. It was warm, just barely cool against his skin.

Ginger breathed in his scent, delighting in the liquid sliding slowly up their joined bodies, enclosing them in a world where their strengths became equal. When he released her she positioned herself against him so that they were joined again. She wrapped her arms around his neck as he took them deeper into the lake. The level was at her breasts before he stopped.

Michael stared at the peaks as they alternately lifted above the tiny waves caressing them, then sank once more. The actions were hypnotic. "I can't remember the last time I laughed when a woman gave herself to me," he whispered. "You please me."

"I'm glad, for you please me, as well." She smiled as she tightened on him again. His gasp matched hers as they rode out the storm of passion together.

Seven

Ginger sat sideways in the car seat, her back braced against the door. "You're smiling," she observed, feeling a vague tenderness in various places to remind her of their passion. Her lips curved in pleasure as she watched Michael maneuver the car over the dirt roads.

He sent her a quick look, his eyes alight with memories. "So are you."

"I hope your friend isn't particularly observant."

Michael sighed, the real world coming down on them in a rush too strong to hold back. "In spite of his looks and his background, he is."

Still having difficulty recalling the man she had only a vague glimpse of, Ginger questioned, "His looks?"

"He's one of the most perfectly handsome men you'll ever meet. I doubt I have a secretary in the home office who doesn't have fantasies about him." He grinned, slanting her a look. "He really hates his effect on women. So if you want to needle him just go all starry-eyed.''

Ignoring the last part of his remark, Ginger pursued her own thoughts. ''I have a friend that sounds a lot like your assistant. It's a shame they can't get together to compare notes.''

''Are you thinking of evening the numbers at dinner tonight?''

''Sort of. Do you think he'd mind?''

''I don't know, but personally I like the idea. If he's busy with your friend, we'll have some time to ourselves.'' He glanced at her, catching the swift satisfaction in her eyes. He smiled, deciding that his woman had a nice turn of mind. ''I'm glad you and I aren't on opposing sides.''

Her brows rose. ''Why?''

''I like winning, and I'm not sure I would with you.''

For one moment she thought he was teasing. Then she looked closer and realized he meant what he said. ''Do I seem so formidable?'' she asked, not sure whether to be pleased or insulted.

''Not exactly, but you don't work in any predictable pattern. I think I will ask my people to check you out better, so I can even the score between us.''

She thought that over. ''You really think that's necessary?''

Michael parked in the drive before turning to face her. Because of the proximity of the house, he couldn't pull her into his arms as he wanted to. ''In some ways, it is. You make me nervous.'' His body tightened as he watched her lower lip pout at him, the need to kiss her growing. ''Keep that up and we'll blow our attempt at discretion right out of the water,'' he warned, unable to resist the urge to move closer. Her soft inhalation told him she was as attuned to him as he was to her. "All I can remember is how you looked all soft and naked in my arms with the lake swirling around us."

"Hush." Her nails bit into her palms as she fought the need to reach out to him.

"I can't." His voice was hoarse with the strain of holding back. "I think we need more than your friend and my assistant in your house to dilute the fire burning in my gut."

She grimaced at the expression, while privately finding its earthy description more than apt. "You know what's at stake."

He sighed deeply, biting down on his needs as he saw the pain he was feeling reflected in her face. "I didn't expect it to be this hard. It never has been before," he said bluntly.

"If you think I'm going to be insulted, you can think again. I hope I'm unique. I want to be so different from the other women that you've known that you don't even remember them." If he could bare his soul, so could she.

He smiled grimly, feeling the desire build at her look of satisfaction. "This honesty is more of an aphrodisiac than I would have thought."

Her breasts firmed, the peaks hardening at the hunger in his eyes. "You started it," she reminded him.

"Next time, warn me what I'm getting into."

Knowing no one could see his hands as long as he didn't raise them above the level of the windows, he risked slipping his hand under her blouse. Her stomach was warm, firm, her muscles rippling with anticipation. He stroked her lightly, savoring the satin warmth as he watched her eyes cloud with desire. Her lips parted as he widened the circles he traced on her skin. He leaned toward her as a soft moan broke from her, straining the bounds of his control. One kiss was all he would take, a taste to hold them both. His mouth brushed hers, his tongue easing between her lips as his fingers slipped lower to the small valley between her legs. He inhaled deeply, finding her damp and as eager for his touch as the first time he had made her his. Heat pooled within him, his body tensing against the edges of control. He wanted her, more than he had ever wanted any woman. His kiss deepened as he probed the secret depths, giving her pleasure, feeling her tighten around his hand, holding him, even as she thrust to meet his caress.

"You *are* unique and I don't know what I'm doing," he breathed harshly, trying to remember where they were. "Help me."

Ginger opened her eyes at the rough command. His face was sharply defined by passion. His eyes burned with the same fiery demand that was turning her body to a living thing with a mind of its own. "I can't," she whispered, moving against him, hating the clothes that held them apart. "It's never been like this for me."

"I only meant to give us a little pleasure." He took her mouth again, a substitute for the mating with her body he craved. Her tongue met his, eagerly joining in a duel that left them breathing heavily when Michael lifted his head.

"A little pleasure," she said, pushing her words out between tiny gasps. "A lot of pleasure." She moaned softly when his fingers probed deeper, teasing forays that set off a trail of fire.

"I love that sound."

Her eyes held his as she began a tender retaliation for his foreplay. Her fingers found the throbbing center of his desire, tracing the outline shielded by fabric until he was as much a prisoner of passion as she. His groan of need made her smile.

"Yours pleases me greatly, too," she teased huskily.

Michael knew he was balanced on the edge of the point of no return. He had to release her or make her his once more. Closing his eyes for a moment, he sought the strength to let her go. She deserved better than the cramped confines of the car. "You play a mean game, woman," he whispered as he slowly began to withdraw his hand. Her skin was slick with passion's dew. Her scent was rich, beguiling and demanding at the same time.

"I wasn't playing." Ginger felt Michael's tension, recognized the needs driving him to complete what he had started. In that moment she admitted to herself that she would have given him all that he asked without caring where they were or who might see. For the first time in her life, she wanted something and someone without counting the cost. She saw his decision to leave her even as he made it. Her body cried a silent protest as she sighed, forcing her hand away from his body.

"That's what makes it so damn erotic. Woman, you are more than I knew existed." If he could just concentrate on the words, he might be able to forget his unassuaged longing for fulfillment. "You make me forget civilized behavior, and that's not my style."

"You aren't alone in that."

"That's the only thing keeping me sane." He cupped her breast, lightly teasing the nipple before he withdrew from her warmth completely. "Will you come to me tonight?" He asked the question he had promised himself that he would not speak.

"If I can."

Their eyes met, both understanding the stakes, both hating the game.

"If there were no one else I'd sign that damn paper and have done."

She shook her head, trying to measure her breathing. The need to give herself was slowly easing as reason took precedence once more. "No, you wouldn't. You don't trust me that much. That's your body talking, not your mind." His hand moved in sweet punishment of her perception.

"Damn you for seeing me too well. It sounded good." He was not truly disappointed, but rather proud.

"I see myself, so it's not so very hard to know you." It was her turn to retaliate with a teasing touch for the words between them. His groan was torture and delight.

"Besides, what's between us is just beginning. You'll owe me a contractor and money if you accept my deal." She was coming close to the edge yet again, the needs building higher and stronger with every word. Bellwood Ridge looked over her shoulder, while Michael stared into her eyes. Ginger knew he could have her here, in full view of her heritage, and she would give herself to him with the same lack of reservation she had at the lake. She didn't fully understand how she could take the risks that he represented, but she had no intention of denying herself or him for as long as the fire burned between them.

Michael felt the change in her body, realizing he had almost brought her too close to the edge for her to hold back. He wanted to feel her come apart but he respected her too much to take her here, as though she were only a body for his pleasure. His hands gentled, soothing rather than exciting her.

"Easy, honey," he murmured, damning his need as he cupped her breasts. "I should have known touching you again, with us like this, was a fool's mistake." He watched the glow fade from her eyes as her own touch softened to a gentle caress. The nails of desire blunted until they finally granted them release.

Ginger leaned back, taking a deep breath and releasing it slowly. His apology was more than she expected—and unacceptable, as they were both responsible. "That wasn't the smartest thing *we* could have done."

The emphasis on the plural wasn't lost on Michael. He smiled, surprised to find it easy. "Agreed." Michael was working on his own breathing.

"I don't think we'd better repeat it."

He studied her, admiring her courage and her honesty. Her eyes were clear, bright and determined. "I don't think I could pull back very often without going stark, raving mad," he admitted wryly.

She laughed softly, liking his ability to see humor in their situation. His earthiness appealed to her, as well. "We can't have that, at least not before we get my recreation center built."

"And my factory." He smiled at her, finding the gesture easier with each one. He couldn't remember a time when the stakes had been so high and he had been so capable of enjoying himself. Ginger was sunlight in a life he hadn't known was shadowed by the gray flannel of the business world he inhabited. Suddenly, he wanted to forget business and just feel, if only for a little while.

"For now let's forget about both our dreams. Let's just deal with the offer you've made. If I sign, we'll handle the next set of problems as they arise. I'm tired of staying six jumps ahead of my life. I want to relax a little." He glanced at the house lazing in the sun before them. "Maybe this place is getting to me."

Ginger grasped the suggestion dubiously, although she wanted to agree more than was wise to say. "Can you be happy doing that?"

"I'm going to give it a damn good shot." He took her arm as they got out of the car and tucked it in the crook of his elbow. In Baltimore, he probably would have gotten a lecture on the gesture. Here, it seemed right and necessary. "I laid on that quilt with you at my side and learned something today." He smiled at her knowing look. "Besides..." The curiosity flickered to life in her eyes. His smile deepened with satisfaction. "I've never had a vacation. I've never done anything without a purpose, and I've never smiled as much in a week as I have with you this morning. I liked it. Do you have any idea what that means to me?"

They mounted the steps together. Before Ginger could answer, Tilly met them at the door.

"I was beginning to think you two were going to sit in that car all day." Her glance took in their closeness without comment. "Lunch is on the table and your assistant is closeted in the back study. He says he doesn't need anything." Her voice gave a clear indication of her opinion of that excuse.

Michael released Ginger with a sigh. Although he wanted to be with Ginger, he didn't want to cause problems in her home. "I'll speak to him."

The moment the two women were alone, Tilly spoke in a softer tone, one carrying a nuance that Ginger didn't understand. "Your godfather called. He wanted you to call him right back."

"Is there a problem?"

Tilly hesitated, glancing down the hall. "Not that I know of," she said without meeting Ginger's eyes. "You go make your call while I get lunch on the table."

Ginger stopped her from leaving with a hand on the housekeeper's arm. "About Michael," she murmured, determined to get to the bottom of Tilly's strange attitude with Michael.

Tilly patted her hand. "Honey, I like him." At Ginger's startled expression, she added, "From what I've heard of him from your godfather, he's a good man. And you're a grown woman. So don't you worry about anything."

"But what about the gossip?" Ginger was bewildered about Tilly's apparent stamp of approval.

Tilly sighed deeply, her bosom rising, then settling into a stately pose that matched her expression. "Anyone who throws mud better be prepared to do a lot of washing," she promised in a voice that could have sent the town's hell-fire-and-brimstone preacher looking for a new congregation. She turned away to head for the kitchen before Ginger could continue her questioning. "Now go change for lunch before the men get to the table," she added over her shoulder.

Ginger went upstairs, trying to fathom Tilly's odd behavior. If she hadn't known she could trust Tilly not to be a matchmaker, Ginger would have thought she was scheming to get her and Michael together. She shrugged, realizing she was probably just being overly sensitive where her intense feelings about Michael were concerned.

Charles scanned his copy of the agreement, which Elizabeth had produced after lunch. The terms were clear, demanding and immediate. "Does she mean to hold us to the letter of this or have we got a bit of leeway?" he asked when he finished. He and Michael had retired to the study after the meal to discuss the terms of the sale.

Michael leaned back in the chair and stared out at the rose garden spread before the long windows. Sun spilled into the room, warming the dark wood and highlighting the antiques that graced the furniture. "She'll hold us to them, believe me. The lady is sharp, and she isn't the type to put something on paper and then change the terms." He could feel Charles studying him, but he didn't look his way.

"You two seemed close for having just met."

"That's just your imagination."

Charles's eyes narrowed. "I don't think so," he said slowly.

Michael angled his chair in a lazy arc. "If you have something to say, say it."

"This whole set-up confuses me. First, her godfather says he'll sell a parcel of land to us. Then he starts throwing up roadblocks. Then, I get a call to come down here, I thought to discuss finalizing the deal. Instead I get a bunch of polite hogwash from a man who is known to be as sharp as a tack. He says he wants to see you. So you tackle the cagey devil and he admits that because of some bequest arrangement he's already sold the plot to his goddaughter. His explanation sounds plausible enough but there's too many holes in it to suit me. For one, he could have told us about the bequest as soon as Elizabeth approached him. He didn't, and given his reputation I have to wonder why. Then along comes Elizabeth to offer you a piece of property that just happens to be for sale when it's *never* been on the market before."

"Get to the point, Charles," Michael commanded.

"You'll think I'm crazy, but I think you might just have been lured here to meet Elizabeth." He held up a hand when Michael looked ready to interrupt. "I have the report from our people now. It seems Elizabeth's father spent a considerable amount of time and money looking for a son-in-law."

Michael laughed harshly, his disbelief evident. "I know all that and I didn't need our team to tell me. The lady did herself and, believe me, nothing could be further from her mind than what you're suggesting."

Charles didn't appear convinced. "Her godfather isn't a man for making mistakes. You tell me why he made one of this magnitude with us."

"I don't know. I'm not even sure it wasn't a mistake. He is old."

"Not that old." Charles tossed the contract he held in his briefcase. "I still think you should consider the possibility you are being maneuvered down here for personal reasons. The idea fits too well."

Michael studied his assistant. "All right, if I were a conceited man, maybe I'd agree to this. But from what Ginger said, she's had plenty of offers, both legitimate and not so legitimate. Why should she go husband-hunting now?"

"Age? She's not getting any younger for all her expertise. It's well known she doesn't like the corporate scene."

Michael felt doubts building, but he couldn't make himself fully believe in them. He wanted to hold on to Ginger's promise of honesty. "So what do you suggest we do?" he asked, curious to see how Charles would proceed.

"If we want to relocate anytime soon we don't have any option but to go on with the sale. I guess if I were in your shoes, I'd be careful."

"I'm always careful," Michael pointed out bluntly.

Charles leaned forward in his chair, his gaze both speculative and knowing. "She didn't *have* to invite us here. In fact, logically, I'd have thought the Judge would offer, since he's already invited you down here a number of times."

Michael frowned at the reminder. He had been so wrapped up in Ginger that he *had* forgotten the Judge's repeated request for him to visit. "She was just first," he murmured.

"Perhaps, but the Judge is an old-fashioned man. Why hasn't he approached us about being in his unmarried goddaughter's house?"

Michael's frown deepened and, with it, his fledgling doubts. "Good question."

"And while we're on the subject, Tilly is known to be like a mother tiger with one cub, where Ginger is concerned, yet she seems to have accepted you without a question."

Michael stared at Charles without seeing him as he replayed the moment when Tilly had seen him holding Ginger in his arms. She hadn't seemed surprised he realized now. In fact she'd seemed rather pleased. His doubts doubled, growing stronger as he remembered her teasing words and her familiar treatment. And yet on the other side of the scales was the clear look in Ginger's eyes as she spoke of mate-hunting and how she had hated what her father had put her through. The two just didn't match. Either Ginger was a consummate actress or Charles's suspicions were completely unfounded. Until he was sure, he would be very careful indeed.

"You want me to do what?" Caro demanded, pressing the phone receiver closer to her ear.

Ginger grinned at her friend's scandalized tone. "I want you to put on your best casual outfit and bring yourself to dinner. I have someone I know you want to meet staying with me."

"I heard about the fire, so don't get cagey with me, Elizabeth Lenore Bellwood. I *do not* wish to meet Charles this way. It will look as if we set him up."

After meeting Charles over lunch and finding that she liked his rather droll wit, Ginger was all the more determined to give Caro a chance. "Pooh! Faint heart never won the man."

"That's fair lady, and I'm not playing this game. Besides, I don't have anything to wear."

Ginger laughed. "Now that sounds like you. Try that black sweater with the gold threads and those scarlet pants."

"You're crazy," Caro stated flatly, her eyes drawn to her closet.

"You said you wanted an introduction. I'm giving you the perfect opportunity in a way that no one could consider the least bit pushy, and I know how you feel about that. I have an odd man at the dinner table.

What could be more natural?'' Ginger's tone gentled as she tried to persuade Caro to take a chance. Her friend had received more than her share of rejection and tended to view the whole male species with almost as much distrust as Ginger did herself. Her looks had made her a target at such an early age she'd had to develop a cool manner just to survive. Men, when thwarted sexually, had not always been kind in their reaction to her refusals.

"I'm not brave enough. You know me, I'm Miss Chicken.''

Ginger firmed her resolve. "You haven't dated in over a year.''

"I've been busy.''

"Fiddle. You've been hiding.''

Caro sighed. "All right, but not without cause.''

"I know, but this isn't the same.''

"I told you I'm vulnerable.''

"And you're going to be one of four. For all you know, you may not like Charles at all once you meet him.''

Caro thought that over. "You've met him. What's he like?''

Ginger blinked, knowing she should have expected the question. "Sort of tall. Lean. Nice voice,'' she murmured. "Come on, be brave. I promise this will be my one and only attempt at setting you up. The rest is up to you two.''

"Promise?''

"On my honor.''

Caro exhaled deeply. "All right. But not the scarlet pants. I'd look like a tomato in mourning.''

Eight

Ginger showered and changed for dinner, wondering what Michael would say when he saw Caro. She had no illusions about her own attractions. She herself was pretty rather than stunning, whereas Caro was truly a beautiful woman with the kind of looks that had often brought more trouble than pleasure. Ginger had never minded her friend's assets because each felt the other was the sister neither possessed. But tonight, Ginger was honest enough to admit to herself that she didn't want Michael to be bowled over by Caro. Most men were and she wanted him to see only her.

She stared in the mirror, smiling a little at her need to shine for Michael. She had chosen her most feminine silk slacks in a shade of butter-cream that brought out the pale gold streaks in her hair. A matching cream top with hand embroidery and padded shoulders lent an air of sophistication in spite of the simple lines of the ensemble. Off-white high heels on her feet and a pair of pearl studs in her ears matched the understated make-up she had applied. Her eyes glowed with new lights, memories of the time in Michael's arms. Her body was tinglingly alive, sensitive to the moments away from him. Surprised at the depth of her response, she had no defense against it. Only the knowledge that Michael seemed equally vulnerable gave her a measure of security and peace.

Glancing at the small clock beside her bed, she realized she had not heard either Charles or Michael come upstairs. Frowning slightly, she wondered if they were still closeted in the study. Believing they wouldn't be long, she had saved telling them about Caro until she changed. Knowing she couldn't let Caro walk in unannounced, she hurried downstairs, pausing only to knock on the closed study door.

Michael's curt voice bidding her to enter brought an unpleasant reminder of her father. He had sounded just so whenever Ginger had been foolish enough to disturb him. Forcing the thought away, she reminded herself that Michael was a far different man from her father. For one thing, her sire would not have promised any woman honesty—regardless of the stakes. To him, women were nothing more than extensions of men. His greatest despair was Ginger's refusal to present him with a suitable son-by-marriage to run his companies. Fixing a smile on her lips, she tucked the hurtful visions away. She had a different life now, one she had chosen herself. No one would ever use her again. "I thought I'd warn you that dinner's promptly at seven and I've invited a guest to even the numbers."

Michael watched her glide across the room, wondering if he could be mistaken in giving her even the smallest amount of trust. She looked so regal, so untouched by those hours in his arms. *This* woman was every inch Elizabeth Bellwood. He couldn't imagine her eating an ice cream cone on Main Street, climbing out her window for the sheer hell of it or making love with him on a quilt in a field. She'd had twigs and white puffs of clover in her glorious hair this morning. Tonight she looked as if she had spent the day having tea with the Women's League.

Ginger stood close to Michael, but didn't touch him. The look in his eyes was one of speculation, not admiration. She wondered at the cause, even as she fought her disappointment over his reaction. "Caroline Archer is a close friend of mine from Atlanta," she said when neither man spoke.

"Thank you for the thought," Charles murmured finally.

Michael frowned, knowing his assistant was not pleased at the companion chosen for him. He was vaguely annoyed with himself for allowing his judgment to be swayed enough by Ginger to agree to a guest for Charles. "We had better change." He rose, waiting for Charles to leave the room before turning to Ginger.

Ginger touched his arm, puzzled by the undercurrents she could sense. "Is something wrong? I did ask you if it would be all right."

"I remember. It's my fault. I should have recalled his opinion of women invited for him." His attention was on Ginger, not his words. Her hand on his arm felt too good. Her scent was exotic, nothing like the delicate floral fragrance she had worn earlier. This one was slightly dangerous, teasingly unique. Without thinking, he leaned closer, wanting to feel her warmth even if he had promised to be discreet. The door was open but for now the hall beyond was empty.

"He'll like Caro. I promise." The admiration she had hoped to see was in his eyes now as were passion and memories. Her skin burned where his glance touched. Her breasts tingled, her nipples pushing at the silk as though to escape the soft confines.

Michael lifted his hand to her face, brushing the soft curve of her cheek. "Elizabeth," he whispered.

At the name, Ginger froze, the desire ebbing from her body as though leeched away. "No, Ginger," she breathed in distress.

He frowned, her tone slicing through the need. His hand curled around her throat, gentling her when she would have withdrawn. "What is it?"

"*I am not Elizabeth.*" She stared into his eyes, seeing his confusion, wishing she knew how to explain. "Don't ever call me that again."

"Why?"

She wanted to lie, how she wanted to lie. But she could not forget their bargain. She closed her eyes, trying to shut out his face. His image seemed burned in her mind. She felt his arm slip around her waist, offering a silent support she had not known she needed. She looked at him then, her decision made.

"My sire called me that. He hated me and he wanted a son. Every time he said my name, that hatred was in his voice. He would let no one shorten Elizabeth; let no one, even Tilly, touch me in love. Every man that he paraded in front of me called me that name with almost the same inflection. I knew what they thought. Daddy was buying his little girl a man. Fools! He was selling me for a son." The words spilled out, shocking them both with their bitterness. "I'm Ginger. I have no wish to be anyone else."

Even though they were lacking in privacy, he couldn't tolerate seeing her hurting without touching her. Michael pulled her into his arms, tucking her head against his shoulder. "Do you know what I see when I call you Elizabeth?" The sudden rigidity of her body told him just how much a mental whip the name had become. "I see a woman with the bearing of a queen. I see breeding, class and the kind of strength that few of us have. I see the tempering of compassion and the intelligence of clear sight." He leaned back slightly, his hand going to her chin to lift her face to his. "I see beauty. Yes, you're Ginger. When you have twigs in your hair and ice cream stains on a sexy little blouse that give me too many ideas for my own good. But right now, you're Elizabeth. And I like her very much."

Ginger had thought the ability to cry had been burned out of her, but she found out differently. Staring into his pale eyes, she discovered tears slipping down her cheeks. His smile was more beautiful than anything she had ever seen. His fingers traced the path of her tears before carrying the dampness to his mouth. One more wall crumbled into the dust of the past.

"It's a good thing you're going to change," she whispered, her voice made husky with emotion. Feelings and words were a tangle in her mind. She was afraid to be serious for fear she would destroy the bridges they were building between them. "I've made you wet."

Michael hugged her tightly, wishing he didn't see the gratitude in her eyes, wishing he could pretend that he wasn't being drawn more deeply to her with every passing hour. "There are worse things," he murmured, succumbing to the spell her body wove around his. Her curves fit him too well. Even now he was becoming aroused. He was caught, and it was getting more difficult to worry about it. He drew back, dropping a hard kiss on her lips. "For both our sakes, I'd better get out of here while I still can." He set her from him and walked away while he could. He needed an icy shower, one cold enough to unclog his mind and freeze his overactive body.

Ginger watched him go, wondering when her need for his touch would ease. One look from those pale eyes and she felt like melting at Michael's feet. Shaking her head over her reaction, she left the study to wait in the living room for Caro. She poured herself a glass of wine and strolled to the windows overlooking the garden. She had no answers for her own situation so she focused on Caro's problems. She had to remember that her friend was still recovering her self-confidence. Her impulse had put Caro in the firing line of a potentially tough male. She should have known better than to interfere, she reminded herself bleakly. What did she know of relationships? In spite of her loss of confidence, Caro was trying—while she had opted out of the race. As though her thinking had conjured Caro up, a knock sounded at the door. Ginger turned and headed for the decanter on the sideboard as she heard Tilly admit her guest.

"I'm nervous," she confessed on joining Ginger.

Ginger managed a smile as she handed her friend a glass of white wine. "You look gorgeous. That cinnamon-toned lounging outfit is delicious. New?'' she asked, hoping to distract her.

"Sort of. You know me, I can't pass up new clothes. My closets are crammed to the brim. Soon there won't be room for me in my house.''

Ginger laughed, glad to see Caro relaxing a little. "I'm surprised there's anything left in your dress shop.''

Caro responded to the teasing barb with a graceful shrug, her smile coming more readily. "There wouldn't be if my assistant didn't hide the good stuff from me.''

The sound of footsteps on the stairs caught both women's attention. Ginger put her hand briefly on Caro's arm. "Just give him that sexy smile of yours. He'll be so blind, he won't notice that you're scared stiff,'' she whispered as she put down her glass in preparation for the introductions.

She needn't have bothered reassuring her friend. Charles froze in the doorway as his eyes settled on Caro's blond beauty. No one spoke for a moment as the two stared at each other. Both looked dazed. Michael's gaze was on Ginger's face, more interested in her than in what Charles thought of the new arrival. He barely noticed Caroline as he moved to Ginger's side.

"I'll take one of whatever you're having,'' he murmured. One cold shower hadn't even begun to cool his blood. His hands itched to touch and caress her. His body was screaming for release when it should have been at least reliving how good they had been together; should have been satisfied with what it had had. He couldn't remember ever wanting a woman so much.

Ginger poured him some wine. His fingers curved over hers as he took the glass of wine from her and raised it to his lips. She watched him drink, feeling the heat build with each gesture. "This isn't being discreet," she reminded him, pushing the words past dry lips. Her tongue flicked out to moisten the curve as his own traced the spot from which he had drunk.

"They wouldn't know if a truck came through the window and ran over them," he whispered back, giving the blond pair a cursory glance. "That is one beautiful woman, and she's knocked old Charles right on his..." He grinned, biting back a less than polite comment.

Ginger tried to control a smile. "I think I'm jealous."

"You needn't be. She doesn't do a thing for my blood pressure, and I promise you that she wouldn't have driven me to a cold shower. No one's ever done that but you, although the damn thing didn't help at all. I'm still burning up with wanting." The last emerged on a low frustrated growl.

Ginger swayed toward him, not doubting the truth of his claim. Desire blazed out of his eyes, searing her skin until she was supersensitive to his every move. To distract herself, she glanced at her guests. "Do something. They haven't moved," she commanded, realizing that one had yet to speak to the other.

Michael frowned, not liking the interruption. "That man is supposed to have a technique that won't quit but he looks like he's been hit in the head with a dead fish. It would serve him right if your friend tells him he's an—" Again he stifled a graphic description, wondering why he was suddenly conscious of his language.

"Michael!" Ginger said warningly. She reached for her glass, only to find Michael handing her his.

"Use mine," he said huskily. "Since I can't kiss you, I have to make do with what I can get."

Ginger found she couldn't ignore the husky note in his voice. She carried his glass to her lips, drinking from the same place he had. The intimate gesture was one more tie between them.

"I could get addicted to this," Michael whispered.

"So could I," she admitted before forcing her limbs to move away a safe distance. "We can't leave them like that."

"Why not? It gives us the floor to ourselves."

"He's your assistant."

"He's a grown man and she's over twenty-one. Let them work it out themselves." He took Ginger's arm, tucking it in his. He wanted her alone. Since she wouldn't forget about the blond bookends, then he would walk with her in the gardens. The moonlight was romantic, and the flowers wouldn't hurt, either.

Ginger planted her feet. As much as she wanted to be with Michael without interruption, she couldn't desert Caro. "We have to do something. They might stand there like that all night."

Michael sighed, mentally cursing Charles's sudden ineptness. "All right. But I don't like having to take care of people. I'm not particularly good at it. Tact is not my strong suit." He guided her to the silent couple, stopping between them. Maybe a change of scenery would help. "I don't want to point this out, but it would be nice if you opened your mouth, Charles, instead of staring at the woman like a landed fish. I'll grant you she's stunning, but you could at least tell her so, along with your name."

Coming out of his trance, Charles glared at his boss. "Cute, Michael."

Caro shook her head, pink creeping into her cheeks. Ginger caught her embarrassment, and could have kicked Michael in the shins. "You're right, tact is definitely not your best virtue," she muttered, trying to pull her hand from his.

"Ginger, I'm . . ." Caro began, stammering a little.

Smiling with born-in-the-blood charm, Charles stepped around Michael to take Caro's hand. "You're Caroline Archer and I'm Charles Duncan. Ignore Michael. He's a bit touchy because I let his motel room burn down. Although—" he glanced at Michael "—now that I think about it, he should be thanking me for my foresight. That place was abominable and Bellwood Ridge is spectacular." His glance slipped over her, his control firmly established so that all he offered her was a masculine appreciation of her beauty.

Caro relaxed slightly, even managing a small smile. "Thank you," she murmured. "I don't normally act like a star-struck fool."

"I thought I made a great store dummy myself," Charles teased with a faint grin.

Tension eased from Ginger's body as Caro and Charles smiled at each other.

"I knew the man had it in him," Michael murmured near her ear. "There's nothing like bringing out the protective instincts in a man."

"That's terrible, and besides I don't believe it. Tell me when you've ever felt protective toward a woman," she said, challenging him as they moved away from the other couple.

"With you. And before you ask, I like it." He smiled into her wary eyes. "Took me a while to figure out what was happening, let me tell you. Felt strange, too. But then a lot of things I've been feeling with you don't fit my personality."

Ginger felt something inside of her give way at the rueful admission. "You don't sound too worried."

"I'm not. I learned a long time ago not to fight what I don't understand. I stop and wait until I can see the enemy if there is one. Then I fight and I win."

Ginger studied his face, seeing again the lines of determination, the visible marks of many corporate battles fought well. There was a warning in his voice for both of them. "I don't like losing, either."

He raised her hand to his lips, his gaze holding hers. "As I said once before, you're a worthy opponent. I like that, too." He studied his assistant and the blonde, suddenly seeing himself and Ginger in Charles and Caroline. The image wasn't a good one, because it reminded him of the things Charles had said. Michael's doubts surfaced as he looked back at Ginger. Could he have been maneuvered into coming to Lynch Creek for something other than the land? "I also think you're a very complex woman, one whose secrets I've just begun to uncover."

Now what did that mean, Ginger wondered. "I don't understand."

He smoothed his expression, trying to fight the doubts with the memory of her promise. "You couldn't have matched them better if you had planned it."

She tipped her head, studying him. "Do you think I did?"

He gazed into her eyes, unable to stop a mental tally of the coincidences that had dogged his steps since coming to town. "I want to."

Three words. Each an individual knife to cut through the trust she was building block by block. Pain. It was colder than the desire was hot. Her lashes drifted shut as Ginger fought for composure.

Michael saw her close up and cursed his promise to her. "I promised I wouldn't lie to you."

Her eyes opened to pin him with blatant condemnation. "But you believe I would, by maneuvering those two together. What would I have to gain? That's how things are measured, Mr. Bottom Line Man."

Her contempt was an acid wash in his mind, burning through his control and fueling the distrust of the man who had learned the hard way the price of fame and wealth. "I don't know. I just know that nothing in this town is as it seems. I don't trust incongruities, paradoxes or illusions."

Ginger pulled her hand from his, no longer able to bear the contact. "I wish I'd never slept with you," she whispered, hating him for taking her truth and twisting it, and hating herself for believing that he was different.

He drew back, his gaze slipping quickly to Charles and then back to her. "You made love with me," he corrected harshly, only by effort of will keeping his voice low. "And you wanted me then, and you do now. You're as much a prisoner as I."

She lifted her chin, staring at him, remembering too well the gentleness and passion of his touch.

Tilly entered from the hall before Ginger could speak. Unaware of the undercurrents, she announced dinner. Michael stood still, watching Ginger struggle to stifle her anger. His own temper was barely under control. He had to admire the way she cleared the emotion from her expression and relaxed her body enough to turn to Charles and Caro as they joined them. But nothing could control her slight flinch when he took her hand. He felt the involuntary reaction go straight through him. For one moment another kind of doubt filled his mind. If he was wrong, he had just hurt them both more deeply than they deserved; perhaps even more deeply than their desire for each other was strong. He looked at her as he escorted her to the table, but she never turned his way. Her face was averted, as she chatted with Charles and Caro. She acted as though he were not present. Angered, he started to draw her attention then stopped. Maybe it was better this way. Ginger had gotten too close, making him too vulnerable.

Nine

Ginger decided she had never worked so hard to create a hospitable atmosphere. Michael sat silently at the end of the table watching her every move. Caro and Charles, fortunately, were curious enough about each other that neither seemed to notice Michael's lack of participation in the conversation. As for herself, Ginger could think of ten places she would rather have been. The only good thing about the evening was that Charles was clearly smitten by Caro. She studied the pair, thinking their golden looks made them appear almost like twins. Both had blue eyes, and were tall and slim.

"I hope you'll let me take you out while I'm here," Charles said, drawing Ginger's full attention.

Ginger watched Caro smile, her eyes lighting with pleasure at the invitation.

"I'd like that."

"You aren't going to have that much time," Michael pointed out.

Charles's brow wrinkled then he laughed lightly. "I'll find a way. Don't worry."

Ginger sent Michael a look that would have boiled water. If he said one thing to dim the glow on Caro's face, she would personally take great delight in making his life miserable. "Everyone takes a break, now and then," she inserted firmly, daring him to air his half-baked suspicions.

"We're already starting with a handicap. A six-month handicap." The emphasis on the length of time was not lost on Ginger or Charles.

Charles frowned, as Caro shifted uncomfortably.

Ginger faced him, knowing his temper was nearing the boiling point. "I didn't force you to buy the land."

"I haven't taken it yet." He was beginning to feel like a man on a leash held in Ginger's hand. His life and now his business was out of his control. His assistant was salivating over the blonde. Michael had sat back, waiting and watching, trying to give Ginger the benefit of the doubt.

Caroline Archer had all the moves down pat. She had the husky voice, the sidelong glances and the looks to drive a man like Charles rabid with desire. Ginger had aided and abetted the woman. Michael's doubts about Ginger's intentions solidified when he saw the way Charles responded to Caro. With every passing moment, he was losing a bit more control of his business. Already Charles was making plans to see more of the blond beauty, even though he knew how hard it was going to be to bring the relocation in on the time schedule they had set up. Michael needed every man, himself included, with his mind on the job. By the time dinner was over and Charles had left to follow Caro home, Michael was holding on to his temper by a thread.

Ginger watched him in silence, aware that he had become progressively angrier, but unsure of the cause. "You might as well tell me what else is bothering you," she said as they entered the lounge and shut the door behind them. His back was stiff, as he walked to the window to stare out.

Michael swung around, determined to bring his suspicions into the open. "How long did you know that your godfather's land was for sale?"

Ginger hesitated for an instant, not expecting the question. One look at his face warned her not to take too long to answer. Her reply meant something important, although she couldn't think what. "If you mean about you buying the tract, I didn't know until the day I bumped into you. The same day I signed the closing papers for my purchase for the town."

He searched her eyes, seeing only sincerity, temper and confusion, but no deceit. He hesitated, then continued his probing. He had to be sure. "Did your godfather ever mention me?"

She started to say no, then changed her mind. "As a matter of fact, he did. It was about a year ago. He said something about meeting you concerning an investment group he was thinking of getting involved with." Suddenly a glimmer of light flicked on in her mind. She didn't need his stillness to tell her that her words were pointing at some damning conclusion. "Just what are you getting at?"

"That was my investment group. Your godfather sought me out. Even asked me down to stay with him at his home. I had to refuse at the time, although I would have liked to have come." He took a step closer. Charles couldn't be right, but he had to be sure. "Two days later I got word he wouldn't be coming into the group, but that he did know of a small town that might be just what we were looking for. Again, there was an invitation to come and visit. Again, I had to refuse. Charles came instead. Lynch Creek was perfect, he said, and our researchers agreed. We put the wheels in motion. Through your godfather, I took out options on every reasonably sized parcel of real estate going in the area."

Instead of becoming clearer, the situation was only getting more confusing. "I know all that. Get to the point."

Michael laughed harshly as he remembered he had used the same expression with Charles. "I'm beginning to feel like a lamb being staked out for the kill. The problem is, I can't figure out who is doing the staking and why."

Ginger took a step away from the door, no longer needing its support. Her anger and the sense of somehow being wrongly accused lent her strength. "I'm tired of accusations. Get to some facts."

"You want facts. All right. It's well known that you and the Judge want to bring this town into the future. I represent a large group ready to pour money and time into the area." He moved closer to her, his hands settling on her shoulders, pressing through the silk to the flesh beneath. "I came for land, and I found you. Lovely, with an old family name that will die out if you don't marry and breed a new generation. I'm rich, successful, and strong enough not to be dominated by an equally strong and successful woman. Have I lost you yet?'' Even as he was saying the words, he wanted her to tell him Charles and he were wrong.

Ginger inhaled deeply, praying for restraint and knowing she wouldn't get it. His belief in her ability to deceive him cut through to the bone, burning from her mind their promise, the moments she had lain in his arms and the fragile beginnings of the trust she had been willing to give him. ''You think either my god-father or I brought you here to marry me,'' she bit out, making sure both of them understood his accusations. Each word was softer than the last until Michael had to bend nearer to catch the last one. His cheek was a temptation that Ginger was too hurt and angry to resist. Her hand lifted. Her eyes must have given her away for Michael caught her wrist a breath away from making hard contact with his cheek.

''Tell me I'm wrong.''

Ginger sighed. ''I'll tell you nothing at all. I have only one thing to say. You get out of my house. To-night!'' She lifted her chin, staring into his face. She didn't know how she forced the words out. The pain was so intense that she wanted to roll into a ball and scream until the sound burned through to her soul.

''I notice you didn't take back the land.'' He pushed her because he wanted revenge. No! He wanted the truth.

Passion of the body became rage of the mind when twisted by pain. ''I take back nothing. The deal stands. I may hate you and what you believe, but the town still needs your money and the people you'll bring here. I don't turn my back on my responsibilities.'' She turned away from him to head for the door. ''You have an hour to be out of Bellwood Ridge, or I'll have you thrown out.''

Michael caught her arm, swinging her around to face him. "No one throws me out."

She smiled again. "You're on my turf. Don't think I can't back up my words."

If there had been desire before, it was gone now. Her body was strong, proud and unbreakable. He might force her to her knees, but he realized that her will would defy him beyond any pain he had the courage to inflict. Angry though he was, he could not suppress the admiration he felt. And that made him angrier still.

"Deny it and I'll believe you." He shook her once, sharply but not hard.

Ginger didn't resist the gesture. "Let me go," she commanded softly when he had done.

"Honesty, remember?" He wanted to be wrong. He didn't want to think she had set him up.

"All bets are off. Fool me once, shame on you. Fool me twice, shame on me. We have no trust, no honesty, no nothing. Not now. Not ever." She looked down at his hand and then lifted his fingers, one by one, from her arm until she was free. Without a word, she turned and walked away.

Michael stared after her, wondering how something so right could have gone so wrong. He wanted to take her back, whether she had done what he suspected or not. They would be together. What would it matter? But he knew himself too well. He had to be able to trust. She had hurt him when he had thought himself too secure to be hurt. Watching Charles being maneuvered by Caroline had been like looking at himself being taken in by Ginger. He couldn't afford the risk. Shaking himself free of his doubts, he left the room, his expression a grim mask. He had an hour. He needed ten minutes. Briefly, he wondered when—or if—Ginger would send Charles packing. He also wondered why he was even considering letting Charles stay.

Ginger sat down on the bed, trying to still the shaking in her limbs. Tears rolled from her eyes so swiftly that she didn't bother to wipe them away. She simply sat as time moved on without her; staring out a window she couldn't see, looking back over the terrible scene in the living room. She had never tried to hit anyone for any reason in her life. That she could so lose her temper, shocked her to her very soul. That Michael would have made love with her, promised her honesty and accepted her own truth in return, was more betrayal than she could bear. And to accuse her godfather, the one man who had not ever used or manipulated her, was beyond anything she could handle. So she had exploded, said things better left unsaid and hurt the man she loved.

She froze, the knowledge sliding into her heart, almost stopping it. She loved Michael. She hadn't meant to, hadn't even known she was capable of trusting any man enough to love him. "What have I done?" she demanded of the empty room. She rose, her hands shaking, her heart pounding. Her pride and her past had cost her something she might not be able to replace. She had to go to him. The sound of a car pulling out of the drive, drew her to the window. The floodlights were nearly as effective as the sun.

It was Michael, leaving as she had told him to do. Her shoulders slumped, her eyes brimmed as the sobs that had not come before broke through what was left of her control. Sinking to the window seat, she leaned her head on her arms and cried as she had not done since the day she learned how little she meant to her father as a person. When there were no more tears left, she still lay without moving. Charles returned, the lights were switched off and the moon turned the land to silver. She didn't notice. Nor did she see the dawn draw back the veil of night as Bellwood Ridge stirred to a new day.

Finally, the sounds of the household awakening penetrated her stupor. Lifting her head, she glanced at the clock on the bedside table. Her godfather should be up by now. She had to talk to him, discover how Michael could have gotten the idea that he had been manipulated into coming to Lynch Creek for her sake. She made the call, having no idea how to broach the subject with her godfather. He had liked Michael, she remembered, on recalling the conversations they had shortly after the first meeting.

"What do you mean he isn't there?" Ginger demanded of the housekeeper a moment later.

"I'm sorry, Miss Elizabeth. But he decided he wanted to take a cruise in the Caribbean to get away from the terrible heat. He left yesterday. Right after the lawyer left with the papers for the land sale. I'm sure he told me that he had contacted you about his plans."

Ginger frowned, disturbed and uneasy at this new wrinkle in her usually predictable godfather's behavior. "What ship is he on?"

There was a small silence, and then the woman admitted, "I don't know. He told me to call you if there were any problems here."

Ginger sat down, having a horrible feeling something was terribly wrong. "You have no contact number at all?"

"No. Did I do something wrong?"

Ginger roused herself enough to set the housekeeper's mind at rest before breaking the connection. The longer she thought, the more she remembered.

"Well, daughter of my heart. I met someone last night that I think you would like. Name's Michael Sheridan. He's nearly as blunt as you and I promise you he's got more business sense than most. Came up from the ranks, too, and doesn't suffer fools gladly. Liked the man. Might just do business with him."

The Judge had watched her closely. She had thought it odd, at the time, but had put his intense expression down to the prospect of a new venture. "I might be interested in a new investment," she had responded casually.

"Is that all you can say?"

"What do you want me to say?"

"Most women would have asked about the man."

She should have sensed something then, but hadn't. She almost smiled at her own naíveté when she had replied. "You know that isn't my thing. I've spent years escaping one grasping male or another."

"You've grown too cynical, my girl. I don't like it—and where is our name going to be if you die an old maid?"

She had laughed, she recalled, not taking him seriously.

"I was a fool. I should have seen it coming. All that hogwash about being guilty for taking Michael's property." She rose and paced the room, not knowing what to do. Michael would never believe she had had nothing to do with her godfather's plot, especially after the way she had fallen into his arms like a woman ripe for sex. Disgust and anger warred for supremacy. She had trusted her godfather, and he had used her. Once more the Bellwood-Lynch name had cost her more than she could afford to pay. She wanted to run, but more importantly she wanted to find the Judge and show him what he had done. But she was caught on both counts. She couldn't leave until the recreation center was complete, and she didn't know where her godfather was. Knowing his cunning, she had no doubt that he wasn't in the Caribbean.

And Michael had as little reason to trust as she. He would not believe her, even if she could force herself to seek him out. The lines had been drawn between them. There was no going back. Squaring her shoulders, she stopped the useless pacing, and pulled off her clothes. The first thing she had to do was shower and dress for the day. Then breakfast and a meeting with her lawyer for the paperwork on the recreation land. She would take one step at a time and forget what could not be.

Charles was at the breakfast table when she entered. He looked up to nod politely. "I hope you don't mind if I started without you. Michael left a note in my room to say that he had to go back to Baltimore to settle some kind of emergency. But I suppose you know all about that?"

Ginger didn't betray her knowledge of the real reason for Michael's departure by so much as a blink. "I know he had to leave." She sat down and began lightly filling her plate.

Charles hesitated, then spoke again. "I don't want to impose. Are you sure you won't mind having me here while I get this project off the ground?"

She raised her eyes to his. "The house is very large and I don't mind the company."

His smile was slight, the first hint of friendliness seeping through. "I'm glad." He tucked into his own breakfast.

For a short while neither spoke, both satisfying their hunger. When they were on their third cup of coffee, Ginger noticed him giving her speculative looks. "Something wrong?" she asked finally.

He shrugged, showing faint discomfort. "I wanted to ask you something, but I'm not sure how to put the question."

"Straight, usually works best." Curious, she watched him hesitate.

"Caro told me that she had mentioned seeing me earlier in the year."

Ginger's brows raised at Caro's openness, but she said nothing.

"I like your friend. I want to see more of her without the polite trappings of making an extra at dinner. Will that cause a problem?" The easy charm that had captivated Caro was nowhere in evidence now. All that Ginger could see was a sincerity that held hope for Caroline's future. "We have a lot in common," he added when Ginger didn't speak. "We get judged on our looks too much. We're sensitive about it."

While her matchmaking attempt seemed off to a good start, she was in no mood to continue the occupation. "That was the beginning and end of my attempts at matchmaking. The rest is up to you two."

He sighed, clearly relieved. "I like her, but I don't know if I could have stood being hunted," he admitted a little sheepishly. "I may sound like a conceited fool, but I'm tired of being stalked by every woman I'm introduced to with marriage or lust on her mind. I can't help what I look like."

Ginger grinned, beginning to like Charles when she hadn't been curious enough to look beyond his role in Michael's life. "We can always call Bellwood Ridge no-man's-land, a kind of neutral territory."

He laughed, relaxing completely. "Sounds good to me."

Ten

―――

"Are you sure you won't change your mind?'' Caro
asked.

Ginger looked up from the computer screen and
smiled at her friend. ''No, I won't play chaperon to
you and the gorgeous Charles. Go have your picnic or
whatever, and leave me to slave away in peace.''

Caro protested, a worried frown on her face. ''But
you haven't taken a break in two weeks. The recreation project is coming along beautifully. That contractor Michael sent down is really something. Surely,
you can afford to sit back for one day.''

Ginger stifled an oath. How could she explain that
watching the relationship growing between Caro and
Charles was only intensifying the pain of lying awake
nights reliving the moments she had spent in Michael's arms? With the exception of the contractor
who had shown up at her door to announce that Mi-

chael Sheridan had hired him to build the recreation center, she had heard nothing from Michael. Nor had there been any reply to the message she had sent thanking Michael for the lower price that he had negotiated with the construction firm. His silence was complete, and more painful to handle with each day.

"I don't want to take a break. You should know by now that I thrive on hard work," she said finally.

"I can tell," Caro muttered. "You've got circles under your eyes that weren't there a few weeks ago. You've lost weight. And I don't care if you tell me until you're blue in the face you're on a diet, I won't believe you."

Ginger's temper was anything but stable these days. Anger rose before she could stop it. "Back off, Caroline. I love you like a sister, but I'm all right. Stop mothering me."

Caro's face closed up at the stinging comments. Ginger regretted the words the instant they flew from her tongue.

"It's Sheridan, isn't it?"

Ginger sighed deeply, not prepared to discuss Michael with anyone. "Please, Caro." Her voice was gentler now.

"Is it because of Charles and me? I know you told me it wasn't, but I can't forget how angry he seemed to be that night. I even asked Charles about him," she confessed.

Ginger's need to know overrode her intention to play down Michael's abrupt departure. "What did he say?"

"He said that Michael has a real thing about women. Since he made it big, he's been chased like you wouldn't believe. Some of them were even ones who wouldn't give him the time of day when he was just starting out. Charles says the same is true for a lot of the men he does business with. They didn't want to know his name when he was struggling and now they're all over him like fleas on a dog, since he came out on top. Charles says he hates users."

"We all do. You've had your bouts with it, and so have I," Ginger pointed out, wanting an end to the conversation. She glanced back at the computer screen hoping Caro would take the hint.

"He made it sound as though Michael believed you were trying to trap him or something." She frowned anxiously, studying Ginger. "I just don't understand what could make him think such a thing after meeting you. Even if you were the type to stalk a man, you don't need to. You have money and power."

"But I don't have a husband." The words escaped before Ginger could stop them.

Caro's eyes widened in shock. "But you don't want one. You've told me that a hundred times."

Since she had come so far, Ginger found she needed to air her suspicions. "He thinks the Judge set him up for me to look over."

Caro dropped into a chair, her face blank with amazement. "But he wouldn't do that to you. Your father would have, but not the Judge."

"I want to believe that, but the circumstances of the property sale are a bit strange. And now the Judge has taken off without letting me know the reason he was leaving."

"That's not much to go on," Caro pointed out dubiously.

Ginger sighed, propping her elbows on her desk. "I keep hoping I'll hear from the Judge, but I haven't. I need to look him in the eye and hear him tell me that he didn't arrange this."

Caro reached across the desk to lay her hand on Ginger's arm. "He wouldn't do this to you. I know it. Michael has to be wrong. I can't believe he thought all this up without help. I saw the way he was looking at you and I've watched you since he left. You wouldn't be this torn up if there wasn't something between you. I would love to get my hands on the fool who put the idea in his head anyway."

"I'd rather you didn't," Charles said, coming into the room. "I'm sorry, but I was eavesdropping. You really didn't know, did you?" He looked at Ginger, his expression conveying his need to know.

Ginger stared back, a horrible feeling of betrayal settling in the pit of her stomach. There was too much knowledge in Charles's eyes. "I wondered why he let you stay. A spy in my house." Her fists clenched in anger at the thought.

Charles withstood her anger and returned it half measure. "I'm not a spy and he didn't ask me to stay. You don't know him at all if you can think that. He doesn't work that way."

"I hardly think you would admit it if he did."

"Stop it, both of you. What are you talking about, Ginger? Charles wouldn't spy on you. You know he's here to head the factory project. He even helped you get the playground equipment shipped in when it got lost."

"Actually I didn't. Michael did."

"How did he know about it?" Ginger demanded, determined to have the truth.

"He knew because I told him. I have been sending him reports on both jobs since the beginning. He left instructions in the letter and has reinforced them since. I am to give you whatever help you need.''

Her pride wouldn't let her accept aid from a man who could believe her capable of lying and manipulating him. "I don't want, nor will I accept, his charity."

"Tell it to him, not me. I only work for the man, and I'm not going against him for anyone while he is in the mood he's in." Charles crossed to Caro and took her arm. He paused on the way to the door. "I don't make a habit of butting into Michael's business, but I will this one time. It was I who had the idea of what I thought you and your godfather were up to. I've had my own taste of being hunted and I didn't want him in the same trap. I know now that I was wrong and I'm more sorry than I can say that I let my own experiences influence me. If I could change..."

Caro pulled her hand from Charles, her face set. "How could you?" she demanded angrily, interrupting him. "The last thing in the world Ginger would do..."

Ginger pressed her fingers to her temple, feeling another headache build. "Don't fight over this, either of you. Let it go. Michael and I will solve our own problems. There's been enough meddling to last us all a good while. Please, just go. I really need to be alone."

Neither of the pair was happy, but they left Ginger in the study. Ginger rested her head in her hands and tried to think. Why would Michael have told Charles to help her? It would have been much more natural for him to wish her ill, unless he was remembering what she had said about winning over the opposition to his expansion by involving himself in important town issues. She frowned at the thought. She didn't want him to have a business motive, she realized. Images of Michael holding her in his arms, his smile when she had teased him, even his anger when she had splattered him with the ice cream returned to haunt her. She had seen his eyes icy with rage and soft with tenderness. She had known his passion, shared his honesty and been branded by his accusations.

Whom should she believe? Her emotions were in such a tangle that she could no longer sort truth from fantasy. Should she trust Michael, to whom she had given her body and love, or the Judge who had been the only fatherly influence she had ever known? Even now she couldn't bring herself to completely accept the Judge had set her and Michael up. But her godfather was gone, without leaving word. That had to count for something. Frustrated, she reached for the phone. Maybe today the Judge's housekeeper would have some news.

Michael sat in his apartment high above the hot, muggy city streets. No sound marred the stillness. No light disturbed the interior darkness. He stared out over the Baltimore skyline, nursing the whiskey in his glass without really tasting it. He was tired, but if he slept he would not rest. His dreams would be filled with Ginger, her warmth, the desire that even now was twisting like a live thing in his body, demanding fulfillment from the woman who had promised truth and delivered lies.

Work, the panacea for all his frustrations in the past, was not solving his problems this time. No matter how much he crammed into a day, the nights were measured in the steady drip of minutes. He had been a fool. Only an out-of-control youth allowed his libido to rule his body and his mind. He had taken her, too lost in his own raging need to see the trap spread so invitingly open. He had been an easy mark for the Judge to cut from the male herd as a mate for his goddaughter. He laughed harshly, a black humor on him. He had been so wrapped up in business and desire he hadn't seen anything beyond that slim body with the mind that intrigued him too much and the second chance for the achievement of his professional goals.

He lifted his glass to his lips and downed the last swallow. The liquor burned his throat, but he didn't mind. He needed the heat in his belly to rise high enough to incinerate her memory. Dropping the glass on the carpet beside the chair, he rose and made his way toward his room. He would sleep because he had to and he would forget because there was no other way to survive.

"Well, how is our plan going?" The Judge settled back in the chair, the phone pressed to his ear.

"It's not," Tilly replied in frustration, glancing down the hall to watch for anyone who might overhear her conversation. "Where are you?"

The Judge sat upright, his brows drawing together in a frown. "I'm in a hotel, not that it matters," he replied impatiently. "What do you mean, it's not? I set the stage. So did you. That motel fire was a lucky break that we hadn't counted on. What could have gone wrong?"

"I don't know. All I'm sure of is that Ginger and Sheridan had hot words. Then he slammed out of here and hasn't been back or communicated with her in any

way that I know of." Tilly sighed wearily. "I could
have sworn Ginger and Michael were getting on, just
as you predicted. I was hard put not to jump and shout
for joy watching it happen. It was so fast. It was like
they had been waiting around for each other."

"Cut the gab, Matilda. I know you like reading that
dreary romance stuff, but this is real life. Those two
are a perfect match. He's smart enough to stand up to
her but fair enough not to destroy her. She can give
him the family he wants so badly and the respectabil-
ity he craves. And they both have money enough they
can trust each other. Professionally their marriage
would be a merger that would set quite a number of
people on their ear. The ages are right. I couldn't have
been that far off."

"Well, in all your cataloging something didn't check
out, or Sheridan wouldn't have walked out on her and
that damn project you were so sure would keep him in
town long enough to get to know Ginger."

The tart rejoinder made his eyes narrow with temper. "How was I to know that Elizabeth would drown
him in ice cream from one of those ghastly concoc-
tions she insists on eating?" he returned testily.

"I told you this was a dumb plan. If either of them
ever finds out what we did, I don't want to think what
will happen."

"They probably will suspect eventually, but they
won't be sure. Besides, what else could I do? You
know how little time is left. I tried everything else first,
but they are both so stubborn and so wary."

"I know, but we also both know what's going to
happen if she ever finds out the truth. We both may
end up looking worse than her father to her. Lyle has

more to answer for than he knows. I just hope he's frying in Hades right now for what he did to her.''

"I am not her father, damn it. I care about her and I want her to be happy. She's wasting some of the best parts of herself hiding behind the shield of Bellwood-Lynch Enterprises.''

"She won't remember that," Tilly murmured, her expression a combination of fear and sadness. She sighed again, really worried. "What do we do now?"

"Find out what happened."

"I tried. All I got was Sheridan's note that Charles threw out. Sheridan said something about needing to get back to Baltimore on some urgent business and that Charles was to see to things here.''

"He doesn't do that. He always keeps his finger on the pulse of what's going on in his firm," the Judge muttered, thinking aloud. "What does Ginger say?"

"She won't talk about him. It's as though he has never been here. She's not eating and, from the looks of her, she's not sleeping, either. On top of that, she's burying herself in that study, day in and day out.''

"Damn those two stubborn hardheads. I spent months getting them together. I won't let them mess up their lives this way.''

"What are you going to do?" Tilly demanded, her worry increasing at the determination in the Judge's voice.

"Knock their heads together if I have to. I've waited long enough for Ginger to see to her future. I know what it means to live your life on the outer fringes of a family. I won't let her do that to herself just because her father was an insensitive idiot who never had the vision to see his daughter for the woman she was.''

"You can't make them care for each other.''

"No, but I can at least get them in the same town and hopefully find out what went wrong with my plan in the first place."

"Are you coming here?"

"No. I'm going after Michael first. Never could quite get the hang of how Ginger's mind works. His is a touch easier."

Michael settled into his chair and started going through the mail stacked neatly on his desk. He had a mild headache and he was in no mood to deal with problems, especially since he was no more rested than he had been yesterday. The intercom buzzed at his elbow. Without taking his eyes from the letter he was trying to read he responded. "Judge Lynch is here to see you, sir. He doesn't have an appointment."

Michael's head came up with a snap, his eyes narrowing. "Send him in anyway," he directed, getting to his feet. Maybe there was one problem he would deal with, and then he could have his life back on his terms.

The Judge walked in, his gaze steady as he faced the unsmiling man. He extended his hand, waiting for a long moment before Michael returned the gesture. "An interesting greeting, Michael. I thought we had gotten rather friendly over this last year." He took a seat as though he didn't feel the hostility in the room.

"I don't think I view our limited relationship in terms of friendship of any kind," Michael stated flatly, wondering what the Judge was up to now. "Mutual respect would have been closer to the mark."

The Judge didn't flinch at the sarcasm. "Meaning?"

Michael was in no mood to mince words. "You know it took me a while to figure out just what your little sleight of hand with that land was all about. You wanted me in Lynch Creek. And you wanted me to meet Ginger. If Charles hadn't suggested the possibility to me, I'd probably still be floundering. Who would have thought, in this day, a man like you would resort to arranging a marriage—or at least that's what I assume you hoped would occur between Ginger and me."

The Judge was visibly shaken at the charge. He sat forward in his seat, his body stiff with tension. "Did you tell Elizabeth your suspicions?"

"What did you think I would do, with the two of you working me like a fish on a string? Go along tamely wherever either of you led?"

The Judge slumped in his chair, his hand going to his eyes. "I never thought you'd figure it out until the 'how' didn't matter, anymore," he muttered to himself. "She'll hate me for this. I had it all planned. You two were alike enough to understand each other and different enough to present a challenge."

Michael stared at him, suspecting a trick. But he decided the pallor of the old man's face was no act. He listened to the heartbroken mumbles, which raised more questions than they answered. One thing was certain. There had been a trick, but not the way he thought. And it wasn't instigated by Elizabeth. The memory of the words they had hurled at each other came back to haunt him.

"I swear to you that she knew nothing," the Judge stated grimly, finally raising his head. "It was my plan and, believe me, she would never have entered into it willingly."

"Why?" he demanded, this time determined to have the facts before he jumped to conclusions.

"Why a plan? Or why you?"

"Both."

He sighed, feeling every one of his eighty years. Only the truth would serve now, and even it might not be enough. "I'm dying. The doctor gave me about two years to make my peace. When I'm gone, Elizabeth will be all alone. No family. A great many friends, but no one who really knows and understands her. She needs so much, but very few see beyond that perfect image she's cultivated. Her father has a lot to answer for, and if there's any justice he'll burn in hell for the way he treated her like a commodity to be sold off for the sake of the family name."

Michael relaxed slightly. He still wasn't ready to forgive the Judge, but at least he didn't feel quite so manipulated. He might believe in love for himself, but he could see the man was telling the truth. "But what has that to do with me?"

"I wasn't at that party that night by accident. I'd been hunting for a month for a likely candidate for Ginger. It wasn't money or power that mattered, although I needed both simply because I believe an unequal marriage is never good. I wanted someone who could need Elizabeth as much as she would need him. I met you, one of the three possibles I had picked, and knew that I didn't need to see the other two. I know my goddaughter. I love her. I saw in you someone who could respond to her and wasn't so blinded by surface considerations that you wouldn't look beneath. I saw a man I could trust, and I don't say that lightly. If you did decide you wanted her, it wouldn't be because of what she had; it would be because of what she meant to you."

"So you dangled the land beneath my nose in an elaborate scheme to get us together."

"I tried other ways, but you wouldn't come to visit and time was running out."

Michael studied him, knowing he was hearing the truth. He had been very wrong, maybe too wrong to put right.

"Why did you leave?" the Judge asked quietly.

"She threatened to throw me out if I didn't," he returned promptly.

He frowned deeply. "She has a temper, but I didn't think she would go that far."

"She was badly hurt." He didn't want to admit what he had been trying to hide from himself.

There was a flicker of shrewd understanding in the look the Judge gave Michael, although he said nothing. "What do you plan to do now that you know the truth?"

"How do I know?" Michael rose and stalked to the window, staring out thinking. "You've left a fine mess in your wake. What do you expect me to do? Marry your precious goddaughter?"

"Would that be so very bad?"

Michael swung around, hoping he was joking and knowing he was not. The eyes might be old, but the mind behind them was sharp.

"You'll find no other to match you so well."

"You can't know that." An hour ago, he wouldn't have considered marriage as a possibility. Now he found the idea marginally less off-putting. He wasn't ready to concede the institution, for him or Ginger. She had showed no more interest in sharing her life with him on a permanent basis than he had. He frowned deeply at the thought, watching the Judge.

"I know better than you think, son. I know and love her, and I learned about you. You're no fool, and you don't make decisions based solely on emotions. Think about what you're throwing away. Think, before you do something that can't be put right." He pushed himself to his feet, his carriage unbowed, despite the illness that was devouring his minutes left on earth.

"Success is fulfilling only to those who don't hunger for more. It offers no comfort in sadness and need, and it doesn't bring happiness." With a sad look that spoke of his own loneliness, the Judge made for the door. "I'll leave my address with your secretary. If you decide to take the risk, call me. I'll stay in town one more day before I return home and try to put back the pieces of a life I may have damaged in my attempt to save it."

Eleven

———

Ginger sat in her car, staring at the recreation center that was slowly taking shape. It was two weeks since Michael had gone. The footers had been poured for the main building, where groups could gather for activities. Picnic tables were being built. Already a few rough paths had begun to emerge, more because of the workers' need for getting from place to place than by intent. The result was a very hazy vision of the completed center.

She should have been satisfied at the progress. The council and the citizens certainly were. Frowning at her own restlessness, she started the car and headed for home. As always, her thoughts centered on Michael. She couldn't forget the way they had parted, or the moments of ecstasy she had found in his arms. Instead of growing resigned to missing him or, better yet, to stop missing him altogether, she ached more with each day that passed. What was he doing? Was he missing her, or was there another woman in his life? Would she make him forget that for one small space of time when neither had remembered the reasons they couldn't trust enough to make a commitment? Did another woman make him lose control the way she had? Did he lie awake nights and recall how much she had wanted him?

The questions were endless and the answers non-existent. Suddenly a bump jarred her, snapping her attention back to the road. It only took a moment for her to recognize the scenery. Without realizing it she had come to the site that she had sold to Michael. The giant earth movers were hard at work, leveling the land. She pulled into a shady spot beneath the trees to watch for a minute.

Michael would be back. He was not the type of man to let the moments they had spent together keep him from realizing his dream or continuing with his life. Until that second, she hadn't thought of the future in regards to his company. How could she live in this small town, seeing him daily, perhaps even knowing his next mistress, and still survive? Yet she couldn't run, either. She had tried that and failed, when her father had purchased her a bridegroom complete with a family genealogy longer than her own and no money in the family treasury. She had run to Atlanta and discovered herself and her ties to her home.

Her life was Bellwood-Lynch Enterprises and the town her family had founded. She swore softly, suddenly very tired of who she was and those who depended on her for their livelihood. She wanted to shop in a store where no one knew or cared who she was. She wanted to do something truly outrageous because she felt like it, and not worry who she would offend or that half her so-called friends were sniggering behind her back. Or make a decision that was based on her personal choice rather than the needs of others. Or sell her vast holdings, pocket the money and live the life of the idle rich, traveling and enjoying herself without worrying over crop prices, the stock market or takeover bids. She wanted more freedom than just the few little flare-ups she had permitted herself over the years.

But she could have none of any of it, for she would not back out on her responsibilities. Perhaps, had there been someone else to take over in her stead, she would have considered opting out, but there was no one. She was truly the last of her line. Sighing for what could not be, Ginger started the car again to head home. She would survive somehow. She always did. A few minutes later, she parked in the garage and got out. Tilly met her at the back door, a worried expression on her face.

"It's about time you got back. I was beginning to think something had happened."

Irritation was instant and difficult to control. Since Michael had left, Tilly had taken to watching her every move. The constant attention had begun to pall and her temper was growing shorter by the day. "I'm a little old for you to be worrying over," she said sharply, unable to hold back the snappy retort. Regretting her quick tongue, but unable to call back her words, Ginger brushed past Tilly to step into the back hall.

Tilly froze, her mouth slightly agape. "Have you got another of those nasty headaches?" she asked, her concern deepening.

Ginger swung around, trying for a more reasonable tone. It wasn't Tilly's fault she was so sensitive right now. "Please, stop mothering me, Tilly. You're hovering over me like you did when I was little. I needed you desperately then, but you can't help me now."

Tilly's face darkened alarmingly. Planting her fists on her hips, she stared at Ginger. "Someone has to worry about you. You don't eat, you hardly sleep and you look like death warmed over twice with those circles under your eyes. You're pining, girl. When are you going to go after that man?"

Ginger's brows rose at the tart demand, her temper taking a nosedive into oblivion. "I am not going after that man, as you so quaintly put it. I have my life to live, just as he has his," she bit out angrily before stalking away. So much for reason she decided irritably as the door slammed behind her.

"A fight with Tilly was all I needed," Ginger mumbled to herself as she stripped her clothes from her body and hurled them into the corner of her bedroom. A cool shower did nothing to help her disposition. Nor did the sound of someone knocking on the front door. By the time the fourth knock thudded more impatiently than the first without Tilly responding, she was past being irritated. She was into full-scale fury at Tilly's apparent sulking.

"Sometimes I wonder who's the boss in my own house," she muttered, hurrying down the steps before whoever it was broke her door down. The last person she expected to find on the porch was Michael. Without pausing to think, she tried to slam the door in his face. He stopped her by shouldering his way into the hall. The small battle had both breathing heavily as they squared off.

"I told you not to come back here." Ginger took a deep breath, and then wished she hadn't. He was standing so close she could smell the fresh scent of his cologne. The memories it stirred were better left forgotten. Feeling her body respond to his nearness made her angrier still. She held onto the temper, wanting it, needing it to keep her safe from the pull she couldn't fight. Deep in her heart there was a tiny seed of pleasure that he had come back. She didn't want to know it existed. Michael had hurt her once, more than she had thought herself still capable of pain. She didn't dare let him get close enough again.

Watching her intently, Michael stuffed his hands in his pockets and tried to remember all the reasons she had for her reaction. He had to ignore the twisting ache buried deep in his body if he was to reach past her pain and anger to the softness he had once held in his arms. "I let you run me off once. But not this time. We have to talk."

The determination in his stance, the sheer quiet of his words was more riveting than any show of temper would have been. "I don't want to talk to you. About anything." She wrapped her arms around her middle, forcing herself to look in his eyes when all she wanted was to hide, to find peace.

"You don't mean that. The woman I held in my arms had too much generosity, too much courage to run without a fight. I'm more sorry than I can say about what I believed." He moved a step closer, watching her intently. "I was a fool. I should have known better and maybe I would have if I hadn't had my balance rocked by one redheaded witch with blazing eyes.''

Ginger studied him every bit as carefully as he watched her. ''You make it sound as though you expect me to accept you back into my life as though nothing has happened.''

''I wish it were that easy for both our sakes, but I know it isn't. We both said things better left unsaid. Apologies are almost useless, because I hurt you as you hurt me. But we can go on from here. Call it a draw and start again.'' Yanking his hands from his pockets, he closed the distance between them before she could object. He caught her shoulders. ''What we have is strong enough to stand against what we have said in anger, if we concentrate on that instead of the hurt. Come to me. Let me hold you.''

His touch seared her skin, but Ginger stood her ground, hardening her heart to his plea. She had to be strong when she didn't think she had the strength to stand alone. Ginger searched his eyes, seeing only her reflection in the dark depths. ''I can't,'' she said, her voice breaking over the words. His heat was wrapping around her like a living blanket. The need to lay her head against his shoulder and give in was growing stronger by the moment.

Michael ignored the words that stood between them and tried to touch her in the only way he thought would reach her. Her body, whether she meant it to or not, was already softening against his. The desperate situation called for a desperate gamble.

Ginger saw his eyes change, her own widening in disbelief as he lowered his head. ''No!'' she protested, turning abruptly to one side, trying to escape his kiss.

His shoulder trapped her there as though he had planned the maneuver. Bracing herself for the desire and hunger she had caught a glimpse of, she discovered instead gentleness and a sweet persuasion that was more lethal than raw power. Her mumbled objections grew fainter as she tried to push him away. The sleeping desire that had never died stirred to life. Her mind fought a brief battle with her body and heart and lost. Her hands stroked the firm flesh she had explored with such pleasure. Her body softened, her need for freedom lost in the feel of their passion.

"This isn't enough," she whispered wearily, her lips red from his kisses, when he finally lifted his head. Her breasts were pressed against his chest so that she was aware of every breath he drew.

"It's a start. I want that and I think you do, too." He glanced down at their entwined bodies. He had been so afraid that she wouldn't let him get close to her. He had come back not sure exactly what he wanted from her, but knowing that things could not end between them. Then she had opened the door and he had known what he should have seen before. He loved her. But what did she feel for him? His fear had doubled, something that would have amused him in other circumstances. Now all he knew was a desperate need to make her his—giving all that he was, in the hopes that it would touch some cord within Ginger.

His eyes glittered with reckless fire. He would have her, taking whatever she would give and building on it. Their passion was a beginning, strong, true, undeniable. "Tell me you don't want me, and I'll walk out that door and never come back." Every muscle in him tensed as he challenged her.

Ginger's head lifted, her eyes flashing with self-directed anger. "Damn you. You know I can't. But I don't want to want a man who could believe I would lie and scheme to trap him into marriage."

He laughed roughly, relaxing as he accepted the reprieve he didn't deserve. One step closer. "Honey, I didn't want a woman who could turn me inside out, either. I wanted some cool, sophisticated female who would sit beside me, never fight me, challenge me or make my blood boil with desire. I got you. A hot-blooded, sharp-minded heiress who has more class in her big toe than I have in my whole body. We belong together, whether you believe it right now or not. You can try to walk away from me, but I'll follow. I'll hound you until you admit I mean as much to you as you do to me. I'll make sure that no man is in doubt that I want you." The need to say love instead of want was strong. He curbed it, not wishing to risk losing the ground he had gained. He had to earn back her trust, to prove that this time he wouldn't fail her. "The only way you'll stop me is to tell me you don't want me anymore."

Want! Ginger was coming to hate the word. Her anger was gone but the pain remained. "It has to be more than that."

"Then make it more than that for us. Fight *with* me instead of against me. Let's build together."

Tears filled her eyes at the dare and the offer behind it. "How can I? What happens the next time circumstances put me in the wrong? Will you condemn me out of hand then as you did two weeks ago? How can I live like that?"

"If you hurt anything like I did while we've been apart, then you won't care what price you have to pay to be together," he returned bluntly, shaking her once. "Look in the mirror." He turned her in his arms until she faced the mirror on the opposite wall. "There's almost nothing left of you. Look at me. I'm killing myself with work because I can't sleep without thinking of you. Tell me a better way for either of us."

Ginger looked because she had no choice. Her heart cried for love, but there was no denying they both had suffered. Michael was right about that. The marks were on their faces and the tension in their bodies. But what of love? She had lacked it all her life. She couldn't settle for less now. She would get over this need for Michael's touch. Almost as if he read her mind, Michael slipped his hands down her arms until his palms cupped her breasts. She watched his face as he watched hers.

"If you can't listen to your mind, listen to your body and mine. We belong together. Logic be damned. The past is a memory that can only hurt us if we let it. Let go of your scars and fears, and I'll drop mine right here in this hall at your feet. Build a life with me."

She wanted to say yes. Her head dropped back, drawing strength from him, even as she stiffened to pull away. "I can't. You believe I trapped you."

His eyes paled, knowing there was no way he could take back those words he had thrown at her. She had to trust him and she had precious little reason to trust any man. It was now or never. "I love you."

Ginger froze, her emotions, her motion and her thoughts all ceased. Her eyes held his in the mirror, demanding, pleading, alive with hope and fear. "You can't."

He laid his cheek against her hair, his expression etched with weariness and tenderness. "But I do. I didn't know it until you opened that door just now and I saw your face. If it takes a lifetime, I'm going to wait until you hear me and believe what I'm saying. I drove down from Atlanta knowing that you hadn't been the one manipulating our meeting." He held her tighter, acknowledging that his confession might very well lose him any chance he had but willing to take the risk. There would be no more lies between them. "Your godfather came to me and admitted that he'd been setting us both up." If he could have spared her this, he would have gladly suffered anything but losing her.

"No! No!" She twisted in his arms, her face torn by emotion—shock, pain, disbelief, traces of anger. "He wouldn't. He knows how I feel about that kind of thing. He has nothing to gain. He loves me." The words tumbled from her without thought. Her hands gripped his arms, her nails biting through the cloth to the flesh beneath.

Michael caught her close, swinging her up against his chest as he strode for the living room. Ginger fought him then as she had not done when he had pushed his way into the house. He ignored her struggles to sink onto the nearest comfortable chair with her in his lap. She immediately tried to slide away. He foiled the attempt. "I'm not letting you up. And I'm not lying."

"I never said you were," she gasped back, realizing that while he was not hurting her, there was no way she could escape until he chose to release her. Refusing to respond to the warmth of his cradling body, she sat tense against him, her head turned away. "You must have misunderstood."

"He told me straight out."

That got her attention. Ginger swung around, her eyes searching his for the truth. "He didn't," she whispered, this time with the dawning of knowledge in her tone. "But why? Why would he want to manipulate us this way?"

Michael relaxed his hold slightly, lifting one hand to brush her hair back from her face. "He felt he had no choice. He wanted you happy with someone who would be there for you. Who would be there when you were hurt or tired. Who would hold you when you needed comfort. Who would love you as he loved you."

Fear sliced through her at his words. The finality beneath them brought a terrible sense of uneasiness. "What is it? What's wrong?"

Michael watched her intently, reading the tension, the fear, and knowing she had to know the truth, but not necessarily all at once and not now when she had so much to absorb. "He is very ill and he's old. He's realizing his mortality and is worried about you when he can no longer be there for you."

"How ill?" Concern for the man who had been almost a father to her drove out all other considerations for a moment.

He could have told her, for he had insisted the Judge see a specialist before they left Baltimore. Having no one else to confide in, the old man had told him what the doctor had said. "That's between him and his physician. You could ask him yourself." Thanks to the Judge, he now knew exactly how bad Ginger's life had been at the hands of her scheming father. His cold-blooded manipulating of his daughter had been as unforgivable as it had been damaging. He hoped for the Judge's and Ginger's sake that she would be able to see the love that had dictated her godfather's actions. Then she could forget her scars and all the reasons she had not to trust men who would maneuver her down paths they had chosen without her consent.

Ginger looked at him searchingly. "You have forgiven him."

"I understand him," he corrected gently. "It isn't a matter of forgiveness." He cupped her chin, stroking her soft skin with his fingertips. "We both love the same woman. I'd do anything to protect you. So would he."

"You keep saying that." How she wanted to believe him. The flicker of pain in his eyes was more convincing than any words. Slowly, she began to believe.

"And I'll keep on saying it every day if that's what it takes to convince you, Ginger spice." He bent his head, half prepared for her resistance. When she lifted her lips to meet him he paused, his eyes on hers, questioning. Her smile was the most beautiful thing he had ever seen. "Say it, please," he pleaded.

"I love you."

"Thank God." His lips covered hers in a kiss that held as much tenderness as hunger.

Ginger met his hunger with the needs she had tried and failed to bury. Her hands slipped around his neck, binding him to her. Whatever he wanted, whatever she could give him, she would do. She had been so lonely, so empty since he had gone. "Hold me," she whispered against his mouth, burrowing closer. His laugh tickled her lips.

"Gladly, love of my life." His hands roamed freely over her back, molding her to him. Her flesh rippled with pleasure, gently stoking the fire that had never died between them. "I want you. I'll want you even when I'm too old to do anything, but right now we have others to consider."

Ginger held him tight, fighting the future that waited at the edges of her mind. She didn't want to think about her godfather. The hurt ran so deep. He had tricked her and Michael. "Must it be now?" she questioned, pressing her head deep into his shoulder, listening to his heart beat beneath her ear. To stay like this always would mean utter peace and contentment.

"They're waiting for us."

"They?" She lifted her head.

He touched her lips, tracing the soft outline. "Tilly helped him," he said simply.

"No!"

"She loves you, too. They hatched the plot and schemed to carry it out. If I'd been the least cooperative and accepted the Judge's invitations we would have met in the normal way when I came to visit. He wouldn't have needed to use all that sleight of hand with the land. The smart old devil really nailed my weak spot. I'm glad he's on our side."

"You sound almost as though you agree with what they did," she accused, trying to come to terms with another betrayal.

"It brought us together. I don't regret that. Do you?" He tugged gently at her bottom lip until she opened her mouth slightly. His thumb stroked the soft inner tissue as he watched her come to terms with the past.

"No, I don't regret us," Ginger admitted with a sigh. "Stop that. I'm trying to think," she added, as his teasing touches blunted her hurt and sense of betrayal.

"I'm helping."

"The only thing you're helping is my libido."

He laughed huskily as his lips replaced his fingers. "I hate being noble and frustrated alone. Besides, I wanted to provide a little incentive for you to make up your mind."

Ginger looked past the smile to the man who cared enough to fight for her and those who loved her. "It hurts," she confessed bluntly. "I can understand why, but it still hurts."

"It hurts because of the past, not because of them," he said quietly, all traces of humor leaving his face. "Lyle was a power-hungry man. He saw everything in terms of use. He never cared about you or anyone. The difference is in the caring. Tell me now that you wouldn't have acted in either the Judge's or Tilly's best interest, even if it went contrary to what they wanted. I know you. When you finally do love and trust, you give without reservation. That's why you're hurting now. That's how your father damaged you so badly. That's why you're so careful with your emotions."

"How did you know?"

"I love you. Maybe, for the first time in my life, I'm seeing with my heart as well as my mind. Now what are you going to do about those two old people whose only crime was loving you? Judge them through the eyes of a child hurt beyond mending by a destructive father or through the courage of a woman of honor, integrity and passion?"

Ginger stared into his eyes, never loving him more. He had given her just the words she needed to find her way out of the past, the pain, the shock and the confusion. "I love them. It's time I forgot what can't be changed and stop waiting for it to happen again. Lyle's gone."

He kissed her then, saluting her strength and her generosity, knowing how hard it was for her to take the risk. "They're waiting at the Judge's house." He rose with her in his arms and walked to the phone on the table beside the couch. He let her slowly down, her body molded to his for one more moment. He started to release her, but she caught him close.

"Hold me."

The last bit of tension drained out of him at the softly spoken plea. "Gladly, love." He turned her back against his chest, wrapping his arms around her as she reached for the phone. He listened while she spoke to the Judge, hearing the old man's hesitant voice brightened at the undisguised love in his goddaughter's as she invited him and Tilly to the Ridge.

Twelve

Ginger turned in Michael's arms, her eyes welling with tears. "He sounded as though he didn't expect me to want to see him," she whispered.

Michael gathered her close, leaning his cheek against her hair. "He probably didn't. He knew the risk he was running in following the course that your father began."

"But he didn't use me the way my father did."

"He couldn't know you would see that." He tilted her chin so that he could see her face. "I tried to tell him, but he felt that you would be so hurt you wouldn't be able to forgive him."

Ginger searched his eyes. "You knew I would believe him? How?"

"We're a lot alike, you and I. I sat in my office and listened to an old man explain his attempts to secure your future. As much a part of his machinations as I was, I couldn't find the anger that could have been there. I knew you wouldn't be able to, either. We don't have many people we trust or that we care about, but those we do have mattered to us more than most, probably because there are so few of them. The Judge has been a father to you and Tilly's been a mother. You wouldn't have forgotten that, no matter what they had done."

His faith touched her as few things had done in a long time. She smiled even as her vision blurred and the tears trickled down her cheeks. Michael bent his head, his lips sipping of the liquid emotion as though it were nectar. "Woman, keep that up and I won't be responsible for my actions," he groaned, his mouth settling over hers to blot out whatever answer Ginger might have given.

Ginger burrowed closer, wanting all that he could give her, his strength, his understanding and his love. Oddly, despite his words, there was no passion to be found in his arms. It was as though he wanted to hold that apart from them, leaving only his love wrapped around her. She lifted her head to stare into his eyes. Her hand crept up to cup his cheek. He smiled.

"Better now?"

"More than you know."

He shook his head as the sound of a car pulling into the drive alerted them that the Judge and Tilly had arrived. "You'd be surprised what I know," he murmured, releasing her only enough to slip an arm around her waist as they walked together to the door.

Ginger almost betrayed herself with a gasp of surprise, as she opened the door. The sunlight fell full-force on the Judge, highlighting his aged features and oddly sallow skin. Tilly looked hesitant. The Judge looked every one of his years, and very ill in the bargain. For one moment, all the tiny questions that still had no answers were solved in that one look. Ginger drew on every bit of strength she possessed to keep her expression clear, welcoming, forgiving. The tears would come later. This time she could trust Michael and herself enough to know only the best possible motives could have convinced him to withhold the fact that her godfather was more than seriously ill. Opening her arms wide, she stepped forward, embracing the pair who loved her.

"I should wring both your necks," she murmured, urging them into the house ahead of her. "But I won't. I like the result of your meddling too much to kick about the method."

"Honey, forgive an old man his need to see you happy."

"You needed someone in this great barn of a house," Tilly said, surreptitiously wiping tears from her eyes as she sat down on a couch in the living room.

The Judge sank wearily onto the cushions beside Tilly, his eyes searching Ginger's. "Is it really all right?" he asked. "I know I shouldn't have done it, but I just couldn't think of any other way." Neither spoke openly of Ginger's past.

Michael curled his arm around Ginger's shoulders, catching his breath as she glanced up at him with all the love he had ever denied as impossible in her eyes. For a moment, the world faded until there was just the two of them.

"It really is all right, Godfather," Ginger said huskily.

"More than all right," Michael agreed, seeing the hint of tears and suddenly understanding the reason.

A swift look at the Judge and then back to Ginger brought a tiny nod. He inhaled carefully, feeling Ginger's tension and knowing he had to help her carry this off. He made himself smile wickedly. "In fact, you two can be the first to know. I want to marry your 'daughter.'" He watched Ginger's expression change to disbelief. "It is customary to ask permission of the family for a woman's hand in marriage?" He glanced at his stunned audience. "The sooner the better. I've been fool enough to wait too long as it is," he added.

"Michael, the least you could have done was ask me," Ginger mumbled, seeing his need to support her beneath the sincerity of his proposal. Her emotions were in a tangle, but one thing stood clear. Without saying a word, he was letting her know he realized she had guessed the truth and would stand by her any way she wished to deal with the knowledge. A woman could go a long way and never find a man like Michael.

"You hush, girl. For a Yankee, your man has fairly decent manners. He knows what's correct and what's not," Tilly muttered, looking from one to the other.

"I've always wanted to give the bride away," the Judge inserted, making no effort to hide a wide grin. "You name the day."

"I think I'd better leave that part up to you. You know enough people in this state to be able to cut through my red tape. If I could I'd make it now, this minute."

"You can't do that. There has to at least be a party to announce the engagement. You don't want the whole town watching Elizabeth's waist when she walks down the aisle," Tilly protested.

"No one better say that about *my* goddaughter if they know what's good for them. Besides, neither of them is getting any younger and neither are we."

"Well, it doesn't have to take all that long to arrange. A woman deserves a little fuss on the day she commits herself to a man."

The comments flew fast and free over Ginger's head. She stared at first one, then the other of those who loved her. Not one of them was paying her the least mind. Michael's diversion had given her the time she needed to pull herself together. Her wedding dress was already under discussion.

"Michael." She tried to stem the flow first with the man who had started it.

"Yes, darling, in a minute," her lover replied, entering into the debate of the merits of an afternoon ceremony in the garden over an evening wedding in the chapel.

"But that will take forever to arrange," the Judge objected.

"No, it won't. Not if all of us pitch in. I won't have Elizabeth married in some old dusty office and that's final." Tilly jumped to her feet and planted her hands on her hips. "Say something, Elizabeth," she commanded. "This is your wedding, too."

All eyes turned to her. Ginger leaned her head against Michael's shoulder, her lips twitching. Suddenly, she could see her future without wanting to cry. Whatever fate lay in store for the Judge, she could give him the fun of planning her wedding and the pleasure of knowing he had settled her safely. "It's escaped your notice that I've yet to say I'll have Michael," she pointed out.

"Well, of course, you'll have the man, even if he is a Yankee," Tilly muttered, looking blank. "Why wouldn't you? He loves you and he's not going to be expecting you to give up the Ridge and he's got enough money to make sure you never want for anything."

Ginger felt the chest supporting her shake. She didn't need to turn her head to know Michael was laughing. "Besides, she's compromised me. She has to make an honest man of me," he added.

Only the Judge hesitated. "You do want him, don't you, honey?" he asked, searching her face worriedly.

"Yes, I want him, but I'd like to be able to say so."

"Then say it, so we can get on to the more important things such as how to do the deed," the Judge grumped.

Michael swept Ginger into his arms. "I have the best idea of all. Why don't I take Ginger away so I can propose properly, and you two set up our wedding. As long as you make it no longer than a week away, I don't much care how it's done." He glanced down at Ginger. "What do you think, my love?"

Ginger touched his face, laughing up into his eyes. "You really trust them not to have us rigged out like Scarlett and Rhett?"

"They brought us together and it looks like that worked well," he returned promptly.

"Good point." Without turning her head, she waved her hand at her two oldest friends. "Do your worst. We have some proposing and accepting to do."

Michael strode from the room and up the stairs even as the Judge and Tilly dug into the wedding plans.

"You're a nice man, Michael Sheridan."

"For all our sakes don't let that get around," he muttered, stopping halfway up the stairs to look at his bride-to-be. "I don't suppose you'd like to walk, so that I'll have enough energy to get on my knees and say the magic words?"

Ginger kissed him lightly, her lips nipping at his. "Out of breath, are you?"

Michael let her down, catching her close when she would have slipped away. Every sign of lightness left his expression. He stared into her eyes, wanting her, needing her as he had never needed anyone. "Marry me, Elizabeth. Make my life complete and let me love you, give you children for this great house and my name to match with yours."

She wrapped her hands around his wrists, her fingers unknowingly settling on the pulse that beat a steady rhythm. "Yes," she said simply. "To all of it and more. I'll follow you if you ask it of me, live with you anywhere. The worst moments in my life were when you left me alone. I don't ever want to feel that way again."

Michael inhaled deeply, awed by her gift. No one had ever offered him so much. "You'd leave the Ridge? This town?"

She didn't hesitate. "Yes."

"For me?"

"For both of us. I've hidden here too long. I'm not the same woman I was a few months ago. I'll always love this place, but it *is* just a place. My home is with you."

He bent his head, unable to deny the need to taste the lips that had opened the gates of his own heaven. His tongue touched hers, finding it equally eager for his taste. He drew her close, feeling her body soften in his arms. For one moment he drank his fill, then he forced himself to pull away. Breathing deeply, he grabbed her hand and started up the stairs, towing Ginger with him.

She laughed as she skipped to keep up. "How good are you at sliding down banisters?"

"Never tried it," he admitted, paying little attention to the question. He had one goal, and banisters didn't figure in the scenario anywhere. He reached her bedroom, pulled her inside and shut the door with a muted slam.

"They're still downstairs," she murmured, going into his arms without hesitation.

"I don't care. Do you?" He frowned, wondering if he could actually control the desire firing his blood if she said yes.

She shook her head, her fingers going to his shirt buttons. In seconds she had his chest bared. "No. They'll be too busy arguing about the wedding. Besides, I'm not ashamed of wanting you. I never will be."

Michael was busy with divesting Ginger of her clothes. "Good." He lifted her in his arms the moment he had her naked, and carried her to the bed. He came down beside her, his eyes alive with love. His hand slid down her throat to her breast, his fingers teasing the peak into full attention.

Ginger arched, her senses filling with Michael, shutting out the world. When his mouth fastened on her nipple she moaned deeply, her fingers twining in his hair to hold him to her. His body was hard against hers as the fire started to build. Michael's hands swept lower, finding the tiny places that stored untold delights. Her lips parted as her neck arched. She was bent like a bow, offering herself to him without thought of pride. He was her lover, the man she had chosen above all others to hold the secrets of her heart, mind and body.

"I love you," she cried in a voice hoarse with need. His fingers danced along her skin, sending shivers of pleasure rippling through her. They tangled in the curls at the apex of her thighs, tugging gently.

"Do you trust me now?"

"I do."

He lifted up so that he could see her face clearly. The glazed look of passion in her eyes highlighted the truth of her claim. "Keep those words in mind, my love. We'll have need of them soon." His fingers traced deeper, feeling the dew gather just for him. His woman was sweet, a wanton in bed and a lady queen to grace his public life.

"Not fair," Ginger gasped as he teased her with tiny forays that only drove the need for his body to be sheathed in hers higher. Twisting, she sought to escape his hold.

He laughed, easily subduing her with a leg thrown over her thighs, trapping her against the bed. He delved deeper, touching the nub that would send her up in flames. Her groan was long, full of a woman's race for satisfaction. He watched her reach for the peak, his hand pleasuring her as she writhed against him. Her eyes opened and fastened on him.

"You'll pay for this," Ginger promised with her last breath as she reached for the summit.

"I hope so," he returned almost gently, catching her to him as she slid down the other side, her body damp from the climb. Michael rolled over, lifting her on top. Her hair spread over him in a blanket of red gold. Her scent swirled around them, mingling with the fragrance of love that hung rich and heavy in the air. He stroked her back as the waves of sensation poured over her. "You're beautiful," he whispered, gentling her.

Ginger stretched languidly. "That was very sneaky," she complained mildly, although she was already busy planning her retaliation.

"I thought I did rather well," he returned complacently, his glance drifting knowingly over her relaxed form. "You seemed to enjoy it."

"And so will you when I return the favor."

His eyes lit up. "Now that's what I like. An aggressive woman."

Ginger laughed as her hands glided over his chest. Although his words were light, she knew they were true. Michael did not fear her strength, nor did he intend to tie her to him. His love and his trust had given her the most precious gift of all, the freedom to be herself. The knowledge filled her with a need to spread her wings, to soar as she had always wanted to do.

Her mouth nipped at his skin, tasting and teasing him as he had done to her. His quick intake of breath made her eyes sparkle wickedly. "You may regret saying that." Her fingers explored lower, cupping him. He arched against her, as she stroked him lovingly. "You may regret this a lot, man of mine," she whispered, her lips chasing her fingers as they roamed at will.

"Damn you, Elizabeth," he muttered, catching fire when he had meant to share with her in tenderness. "Where did you learn that?"

"You taught me the last time we were together. Don't you remember?" she asked, her words reverberating against his stomach. Her tongue flicked out, teasing him so that his only answer was a harsh groan.

"I created a witch," he groaned as she traced his length with her lips. He wanted to hold her, but all he could do was lay there, a willing sacrifice to her desire. And when the peak rose before him, he hurtled toward it, her name on his lips, his hands buried deep in the red gold flames of her hair.

"I love you," she whispered as she rose to join them as one. She smiled as he opened his eyes to look at her.

"You'd better. We belong to each other now and I'll not let you go no matter what the future holds," he promised hoarsely.

Michael watched Ginger dress, enjoying the intimacy of having shared a bath with her. Every move was graceful and the smiles of happiness, bonuses. "Here, let me do that," he murmured as she began to button her blouse.

Ginger laughed, shaking her head. "No. You'll take forever and we should get back downstairs before Tilly and the Judge come looking for us." Her smile dimmed, her expression etched with sadness.

Michael felt the change immediately. He gathered her close, feeling the pain invade her body. "You know, don't you?"

Ginger leaned her head against his chest and nodded. "So many things make sense. Being ill and old wasn't enough of a reason for him to pull something like this. There had to be more."

"I didn't want to lie to you."

Tears filled her eyes and she let them fall. "He told you not to tell me, didn't he?"

"Yes." He sighed deeply. "I had to give him my word." He tilted her head up, his fingers tracing the tears on her face. "I'm sorry."

She shook her head. "Don't be. He's given me so much. I can give him this. We'll play the game his way."

Michael knew what the next months would cost her but knew also that his woman was strong enough to pay the price. "I wish I could make it better for you."

She smiled then, her eyes loving him. "You have. He won't see me cry, though I have a feeling you will. I'm not going to pretend I don't hate this. I'm not brave and I don't want to smile, but I will ... for him. It's all I can give him."

"We both will."

"Thank you."

He shook his head. "No, don't thank me. The Judge and Tilly are your family. I love you and because of that alone I would be prepared to love them as well. But more than that I respect the Judge. He's a canny old devil and Tilly's the kind of mother any man would be proud to claim as an in-law, even if I am a Yankee."

Ginger laughed shakily as he had hoped she would. "You even got the accent right."

"You mean that genteel mixture of disgust and acceptance." He tucked her arm in his and headed for the door. "Smile for me, my love. We have a marriage to attend and a life to get started."

"It's about time you two reappeared," the Judge muttered as Ginger and Michael entered the living room.

A tea tray sat on the coffee table and Tilly was pouring out two more cups. "We have the date set for a week from yesterday. The church circle is on the phone right now, calling all our friends. The chapel is reserved and that designer you like in Atlanta is sending her assistant down tomorrow morning with a selection of gowns."

Ginger sat down in the chair facing the couch, hardly noticing Michael perching on the arm beside her. "You've done all that already? Next you'll be telling me you've picked out the names for the children we'll have."

"I thought Jonah would be nice for a boy," Michael murmured, unable to resist the need to tease—a first for him—but then the day had been filled with firsts. What was one more?

"No, you won't, Michael. I won't have it," the Judge sputtered, going red in the face. "No boy of my blood deserves being saddled with my name."

"Now, Godfather," Ginger chided, blinking back a fresh onslaught of tears at Michael's thoughtfulness. She glanced up at him with a smile, forcing her emotions into the course she had chosen. "I think it has strength and character."

"Hogwash. It has nothing going for it but a built-in way to be harassed by fools. Give the child a decent name."

"Besides, our baby could be a girl," Michael observed, responding to Ginger's need for support. He looked around the lovely antique-filled room. "I think I have a wish for a daughter named Scarlett. It would certainly be appropriate when she inherits her mother's hair."

"You wouldn't," Ginger gasped.

"I knew the boy had guts."

"My Elizabeth could not help but have a daughter with her glorious hair. It's a family tradition."

Two generations of Lynchs, Ginger and the Judge, stared at Michael with duplicate expressions of dismay on their faces. But on the walls the paintings of those no longer there to voice their thoughts seemed to smile.

A new generation would soon fill the house with laughter, tears, problems and treasures. The Bellwood-Lynch dynasty would change and grow with the infusion of Sheridan blood. The sons, of which there would be two, Jonah Michael and Dane Mica and the red-haired, fiery tempered Scarlett Louise would show the strength, courage, power and determination of their parents. But more, they would know the value of trust, love and those people who were close to them, for their values were forged through those of their parents, Elizabeth "Ginger" Bellwood and Michael J. Sheridan.

The stars shone brightly over The Ridge. The moon painted the land silver. Silence surrounded the stately home. A light laugh lifted into the stillness. A man's husky voice answered. The wind sighed deeply, sliding through the trees to caress the earth.

"I did well for an old bachelor. Even the wedding went off without a hitch. Elizabeth was a beautiful bride and Michael knew it, too. Never let the girl out of his sight that day, nor any other after that," the spirit once called the Judge whispered on the breeze as another happy laugh floated from the open window of the bedroom. "I knew theirs was a match ordained in heaven."

Summer lightning struck. The spirit chuckled, not one whit afraid. "So I had a little help from my friends. Only you and I know any different."

*   *   *   *   *

SILHOUETTE
Desire

COMING NEXT MONTH

AVAILABLE NOW:

◉. SILHOUETTE®

Desire™

ANOTHER BRIDE FOR A BRANIGAN BROTHER!

Branigan's Touch by Leslie Davis Guccione

Available in October 1989

You've written in asking for more about the Branigan brothers, so we decided to give you Jody's story—from *his* perspective.

Look for Mr. October—*Branigan's Touch*—a *Man of the Month*, coming from Silhouette Desire.

Following #311 *Bittersweet Harvest*, #353 *Still Waters* and #376 *Something in Common*, *Branigan's Touch* still stands on its own. You'll enjoy the warmth and charm of the Branigan clan—and watch the sparks fly when another Branigan man meets his match with an O'Connor woman!

SD523-1